TAINT

TAINT

A NOVEL

JANET KELLEY

atmosphere press

For Blanka

Success is counted sweetest
By those who ne'er succeed.
—Emily Dickinson

In America we have only the present tense. I am in danger. You are in danger.
—Adrienne Rich

PROLOGUE

"Rebecca," Ms. Walters, my high school English teacher, said in the crowded hallway as students streamed by, "I care about you." She put her hand on my arm and I tensed. "Maybe one day you will write about it." I shrugged her off. Now that day has come. I wrote this story in a frenzy, the memories unscrambling as the words filled the pages.

I clearly remember the day Ms. Walters drew a bridge on the whiteboard. "Grammar," she said, "is like the wooden framework used during construction. When you tear it down it reveals a bridge spanning a river. The finished bridge has to work, but it can also be a thing of wonder, worthy of contemplation." Ms. Walters, wherever you are, I hope this book both works and gives my readers something to contemplate. It certainly is a bridge I had to cross.

Readers, this love story is a necessary fiction. I'll take you back in time when my senior year of high school and terrorism coincided. Planes exploded inside skyscrapers.

Everyone saw what happened in New York City. That same year my best friend was raped in a town you've never heard of in Kansas, the heart of the States. I was the only witness. I felt alone, brave, unbearably sad, and trapped. I loved Luke. This is his story.

CHAPTER ONE

THIS WILL BE ON THE TEST

Luke's voice has a hard edge on the phone. I hang up and yank on the nearest pair of jeans. I slip quietly between the front door and the screen. I am ready to run out and get in his car without saying a word to my mother. I stand there motionless, my hand on the cool metal of the screen door handle. Time speeds up and stalls. Pressure builds in my chest, nagging me to breathe. My head knows something is truly wrong. I feel extreme calm. The deep calm of utter terror. I know. And in the face of the impending doom, I feel powerful. Luke had called me.

In that moment I glance down and see my tennis shoe is untied. I bend down and tie my shoe, a firm double knot, and see my laces for the first time: new, hard tips of plastic. Pristine ropes.

He arrives. The blue minivan rolls into the curb and he cuts the engine. The engine clicks and hums as I approach. When I open the passenger door, before I see him, I breathe in, and then: I see him and forget to exhale. He is the opposite of cool. He is a mess. All jacked up on caffeine,

I guess. His eyes are red, swollen. He shoves his fists deep into the sockets. I have never seen him like this. I sit in the front seat and look down at my perfectly knotted shoelaces. But I don't want to be here. I don't want to see this. I don't want Luke to say anything at all. I want things to be okay. I want to drink coffee at the diner with my friends and use my Bic to pass notes during study hall. But I have to stay. I have to hear his story. He is my Luke. He parks near the grade school, where we both went. The red brick building is smaller than in our memory. The playground empty and dark.

–It was a few days after my birthday. God, Bec. Swear to me, swear to me you will never, never say a word to anyone. This is it, Bec. You and me. I trust you.

Of course I promise, no repeats. And then he tells me what happened.

–It was just after my birthday. Last Friday night. Tiff was at home with her family, I think. Family movie night. You were at the football game taking pictures for yearbook. He called, said a bunch of guys were going out to his dad's place on the lake. Hanging out, beer. Whatever. I wanted to go. I wanted to see the place. When he came by my house in his truck, it was just him and another guy. They said the other guys would meet us there later, they were getting more beer—scoring it from someone's older brother, they said. It was cool. All the way there I was pressed up against the window thinking: Yeah, this is it. This is being alive, you know? It would be us just hanging out at the lake. We were on the way. And the moon was out. And we talked shit. When we got there, the house was dark, and he let us in the garage with a key. The place was all musty, closed up already for the winter.

8

Closed up real early, I thought. Crazy. No electricity, man. But he had a cooler in the truck, and it was full of beers. You know I don't drink much, but I was all weird—all what do I talk about? I mean this was the *Lake House*. I was there. Maybe we were cool now. He was such an ass before. But things had changed, I thought, things can really change and they brought me here and this was cool—the rest of the year things would get cool with them. After all, we're seniors now. It was dark and the beers were cold and I drank two. Fast. Then a third one, real slow 'cause I was starting to feel liquid. Then he was gone, I mean the other guy. And then he was all "you got a girlfriend" and "a hot one?" and I said "not now, man." Then he said, "you know, I remember that shit from ages ago." Maybe I was supposed to deny it or tell him he was full of shit, but I froze. I wanted to run, but I didn't. Steal his car? Run into the woods and be hunted? Besides, even though my legs tensed and I broke a sweat, I thought I could still play it cool. Whatever. Maybe I was just tricked up on beer and all hyper-tense. Then. He threw a punch, not too rough. He said, "did that hurt, you fag?" A fist, this time for real. I was half-crouched down and had my jaw in my hands, the ache, and then my nose starts to gush. I smile at him, trying to make it a joke, smooth it out, and play it off. He smiled back, but his shoulders tense up and he shakes. He jumped at me, wrestled me down. His hands, see? Bruises here and here on my forearms? He says, "see this hunting knife, my dad's" and "see it you faggot?" And then he gets in my face and whispers in my ear, "take off your pants—show me your dick, fag boy." And I did. Then. He had his pants off. Becca, I couldn't breathe, I didn't—couldn't—say a word. I couldn't even close my eyes.

I ran into the bathroom, locked the door. There was blood, a mess. And I collapsed on the bathroom floor. The tiles were cold against my skin. And it hurt, it hurt.

How could I have been so stupid?

–I swear, Luke, you are not stupid.

Then I say nothing, just sit with him in the car and hold his hand. I am stunned into body language. I press my hands around his. My fingers are hot on his cold flesh. My arms grow heavy as I stretch across the seat. My lower back burns, twisted toward him.

HELLO, MY NAME IS REBECCA

Let me try and start again. At the beginning, or at least at the before. Let me try to give you the introduction you need. All good books give you the background before the inciting incident that changes everything. I gave you the terror first. Because that is the way terror works. You don't see it coming. After, your brain eats itself alive trying to make sense of it. Later, you realize how to survive.

I will have to go back in time and begin again.

It is fall semester, 2001, our senior year of high school. We are ordinary kids, normal and brave and good and kind. Also, clueless as befits our rank. Our lives are basically boring. The world is safe. We do our homework. Homecoming and Prom are the highlights of our senior year. We want to grow up and think that getting there, over there, into the real world is a matter of grades and a function of time.

My name is Rebecca. Hello. Luke is my best friend and he is more than my best friend.

My name used to be Rebecca, just Rebecca. There used to be a girl named Rebecca White before it happened.

Before the Lake House. Before Luke told me about that night. Before he told me and then made me promise not to tell. Before I promised. Let me introduce you to her, sweet, straight-talking, fill-in-the-blanks, do the right thing, poem in her pocket, Rebecca Before:

I, (Rebecca Before) order plain black coffee. (Please, with a genuine smile.)

A Kansas diner in the afternoon in early September is a tired place. The waitress plods back to the kitchen.

I extract my spiral notebook and a royal blue-ink Bic from a new 12-count package. My words spill out in cheap ink, flowing thick and bold across the paper, coaxing the edges into curlicues as I fill an entire page with World History notes. I am deep into my longhand and can hear Mrs. Wright's even-keeled lecture voice when the waitress plunks down a pot of coffee, a white ceramic mug and chipped saucer.

The diner's endless pot is why Luke, Tiffany, and I worship this dive. Luke prefers the flavored coffees—hazelnut or black forest cherry. After several cups, things get jumpy: All-over-the-place issues told and retold, embellished stories, perfected memories and far-fetched college plans debated and tabled. We talk and talk (and talk) like the world is a red plastic balloon hot and aloft with our collective air. It burns the lungs to exhale so many words, but at the end of the night, we can burst the balloon and there's no incriminating evidence. No record of our hot-air attempt at youth.

We drink coffee to stave off life after graduation—or *the LAG*, as Tiffany has so-coined it. We drink coffee to edge a bit closer to that world without having to be one of them, the adults. Hurry up and wait for the future where we plan to be friends forever. Really.

We are the Class of 2002. We have waited our whole lives to be right here, right now. We sit in our diner, in our booth, in our moment. Pass the sugar, please.

Luke loves his coffee flavor-of-the-day, while Tiffany rallies us for whole-pie bonding sessions. Tiffany is not happy with individual pie slices. In the dictionary, she says, pie is whole. (Yes, we are those kids—the ones who pull out a dictionary mid-conversation.) While there are 26 definitions for "pie," we rely on the one that says: *A whole regarded as divisible into shares.* Thus, pie should not be divided unless it is shared. Once a month or so we humor Tiffany and order an entire pie fresh from the rotating glass case. We devour it down to the soggy crumbs, even when our stomachs lurch before that last half-slice of peanut butter goo.

No pie today for me. I'll take my coffee without the slice, even though I ogled the banana cream. Luke and Tiffany are elsewhere and I am here in this dimly lit diner for one reason. Well, two. I must ace the first quiz of the year. Then, there is another, more compelling, mission.

Truth: I hate coffee. When Tiffany and Luke are here, I pretend to drink the stuff while they rattle on about politics—high school, family, and occasionally city, state, and country too. I sip and furrow my brow in thoughtful concern. I hate being a sip, a fake. In my deep-down, I want to be authentic with a capital A. The real deal. What you see is what you get. And so I am determined, finally, to learn to enjoy coffee. It is a matter of discipline, a deadening of select taste buds. It is bitter stuff and sugar makes it crunchy. While I adore a tall glass of cold milk, milk in coffee disappoints. I like to swirl in a stream of liquid artificial creamer but always wish I could unswirl it back into two distinct ingredients. The dark and the light, distinct and in their separate orbits. You can't. I've tried.

I give up on World History and pour the coffee, fast and loud, a bit of overflow into the saucer. No sugar. No milk. This is the kind of girl I want to be: straight-up, no dilution, no sugarcoating and no artificial sweeteners or added flavors. I raise the cup with an air of careful nonchalance and meet the gaze of the old farmer-looking guy at the table next to me. My eyes freeze wide as I suck down a swift draft.

The farmer hacks off forkfuls of maple-syrupped pancakes. He fits in this faded diner, the air slick with grease. It is the kind of place that is never full, yet the waitresses are overworked. The manager fires up the ancient vacuum and weaves it across the beige carpet. The tightly woven carpet creeps me out. I once watched a baby barf on it—a hot, fast stream of curdled milk and red chunks landed with a splat.

I tap my Bic down the page. My list started during yet another teacher's welcome back/here's the syllabus/do you have your textbook speech. Since freshman orientation teachers have required us to make lists: homework assignments, life goals, and even TV usage and exercise time. A few minutes to kill during homeroom? Let's chart our life goals!

I abhor turning in school lists for review. Supposedly they are "graded" on the content, which is kept "private." Waste of time. I do not bleed my soul onto a page for my teachers.

Having ranted all that in my head, I admit I love my own private list. I glance down the items I've added and indulge in a little smile. In fact, there are three reasons for my solo visit to the diner: study World History, drink coffee, and contemplate my list. I give myself a mental pat on the back for number one:

1. drink coffee
2. have and use credit cards
3. pay bills (car insurance, et cetera.) on time
4. nod your head and look the person in the eye when listening
5. make "small talk" about current events (must read newspaper or *Time*)
6. don't take birthdays seriously (or have fun at them)
7. write thank-you notes
8. date men
9. be witty (not funny)
10. graduate from college
11. keep your figure (until 30, at least)
12. do not use the word "like"
13. have principles
14. become vegetarian?

I underline number 12 and cross out number fourteen. I add number 15: stock refrigerator with condiments. I hate when we run out of ketchup at home.

And then I add 16: green jeep. What bona fide adult drives anything except a car that realizes her personal tastes and quirks? When we were freshmen we counted down the days until we got our drivers' licenses and dreamed about our ideal cars. Luke once told me that my car should be green because it accentuates my red hair and my "natural beauty." Oh, Luke. At least I am natural.

The jeep will be tough, rugged and designed to climb mountains, forge streams, tangle long hair. I know for sure that I am not a truck girl, nor am I a girl to be driven around in a truck. Yes, I am a green jeep girl, soon to be a green jeep woman.

A Green Jeep Woman—I like the ring of it. As soon as I graduate and master all the items on my list, I'll be free to hit the highways and breathe in all the exhaust I can bear as I find some mountains to scale. Luke will ride shotgun. He'll go along for the ride. It will be the two of us on the road to tomorrow. West is the way forward. I can feel the wind in my hair.

THE FIRST DAY OF THE REST
OF MY LIFE

The alarm buzzes at 5:45 a.m.

By now the alarm has lost the surprise effect to jolt me awake. You can get used to horrible things if you get a pay-off. And there is a pay-off: time to go through my morning ablutions, powders, and such without the need to rush. Without the alarm, my day would be ruined by a disaster of last-minute preparations. I don't do last minute.

I set the alarm every night when I first settle into bed (before I get too drowsy) and double-check it sometimes twice. I take one snooze in the morning, exactly one. I keep the alarm on my dresser halfway toward the door. I launch out of bed, my hot-from-the-covers body unsheathed as I slam the snooze while my brain stays asleep. Then back under the covers, deep. On special days—today is special because it is Friday and I have finished 16 school days (164 left) of my last year of high school—I take two snoozes, but I have to deserve the luxury.

Then hot, hot water in the shower. My back curls under the spray, and then my hands stretch up high lifting my heavy breasts as I lean into arc of my spine—right then left. There they are each and every morning: two ships in the night; islands in a stream. A good neck and spine stretch followed by cracking first my right, then my left knee. I think: no breakfast. . . tell mom get batteries. . . today is physics, world history, English, and journalism/yearbook. . . Jeff in fourth hour. . . must wear chocolate brown cords and the black tee if it is clean and not crumpled in a sad little heap somewhere on my floor. . .Tiff at lunch, Luke will come late 'cause Mr. Dean always dismisses late. . . graduation—valedictorian?—KU or an out-of-state college?. . . applications. . . yeah. . . okay. No breakfast. Then I trace my hipbones and catch my stomach flap in both hands, still there. I am still here. Just before I reach for the tap to shut it off, I summon the courage for the critical question: Shall I skip school today?

I do not skip school. I have never gotten past the question posed in the heat of the shower, but I might do it someday. I should anyway. But I won't. They announce Perfect Attendance at graduation every year—asking the students to stand and face the entire assembly. That will be me. Cursed with good health. Doomed to succeed.

Today calls for sensible soft cotton undies and bra in mint green: no fluff, but, no bother, either in soft cotton coordinating pastel lime. Then lotion smoothed on my calves and elbows. Socks are still optional, weather-wise, and I opt to free-toe it. I have lost love for my cords and go for the black denim. I slip into my clogs for another inch, even though Tiff begs me to lower my stature for my own sake. My face takes a bit of courage: first I examine my zits and check if a new one has metastasized since last night. A bit of base artfully applied and a shimmer of powder may not hide the grossity, yet dramatic eyes and lips can distract the eye of the beholder. Mom took me to the Clinique counter at the Dillard's store in the mall to acquire skincare basics before I debuted in seventh grade. I go for their clean look, but I am not afraid to use the brush more liberally when needed. Mom is Clinique all the way: her face frozen into a mask of itself 15 years younger. The skin under her eyes is coated in bright concealer. Her eyebrows etched in a dark arc of surprise. Her cheeks chiseled by blush. She looks refined, defined, unlined.

I prefer to be behind the wheel and on the open road by 7:15, tuned into Classic Rock 93.7's morning show, complete with riffs on President George W. Bush and the latest on David Lee Roth. Edifying. Stimulating. My head is already there rocking to old school Van Halen when Mom leans inside the door of my room. I stack my books and pens in my backpack—approximate ballast: 17 pounds.

–Anything happening today?

–Regular day in the trenches, Mom.

–You look sharp. That green shirt suits you. Okay, I'll be here at five-thirty. Chicken?

–and rice?

–maybe steamed broccoli too? fine.

She knocks her knuckles against the doorframe and waves as she admonishes,

–Drive safe.

In the car with Van Halen on the radio, I think: paper towels, Jeff, fourth hour, Luke and Tiff at lunch, "drive safe," Jeff, graduation, coffee at the diner—and wham I want a cup of coffee to steam up the car. This is a good sign. Liking coffee is a matter of will and imagination, I think. I have the will.

I step on the gas as I turn into the highway's long curve.

LUKE'S 17TH BIRTHDAY PARTY

Birthday parties freak me out. I have dreaded my own birthday parties since second grade when my mother arranged a boy-girl surprise party that Melanie Parkers told me about during dodgeball. I told her, no way. But I saw the evidence soon enough at home: a series of hushed phone calls and hallway conversations. Then I found a grocery sack buried deep in the pantry, filled with a rainbow of balloons and crepe paper. Melanie had been right. A surprise party. My lungs constricted as I sat down in the cool darkness of the pantry with a heavy heart, no longer intent on finding an unopened jar of smooth peanut butter. I didn't want a sandwich anymore, and I didn't want a surprise party—especially a surprise party where I had to pretend to be surprised. I wanted my mother to cancel the party, but telling her would reveal that I knew the secret. A fix.

I put a wide grin across my cheeks and kept my eyes frozen wide with fake surprise for the entire ordeal. The pictures show me in a blue dress with frilly sleeves, my teeth bared in utter photogenic will to appear surprised.

Mom still reminisces about that party with soft maternal delight.

When I was 12, finally, I told her that parties were for babies. She shrugged at me with a sadness that touched me, making me want to recant my theory, but then I got angry at her tenderness. I watched her turn around and saw her close the door without making a sound. It hurt(s) me to grow up right before her eyes.

I am happy to do away with them—not just mine, but all birthday parties. Tiffany says that I am uptight. She was at my second-grade surprise party and has told me that it was just a party, not a milestone in my childhood development.

–Becca, what's the harm of stupid hats and cake? Chill.

Tiffany is Tiffany. She is loyal and sweet. Her mom and dad are probably the best people I have ever met. When we hang out at her house, there are vacuum lines in the soft carpet. Her mom always asks about my mom. Then she discreetly disappears in the far reaches of the house, leaving fruit and nuts on the kitchen counter. Tiffany adores her parents and when I see her brush her lips across her mom's cheek, I feel part of their tenderness. Tiffany has a good life. Sometimes I think this explains why she is a good friend. She doesn't ask much from me. She just needs me to be myself. I love that about her. Tiffany is sweet and has the best shoes, but sometimes she seems out of touch, to be nice, a bit air-headed, to be blunt. However, there are times that she gets it dead on. And she's right this time about my hang-up about birthday parties. There is no actual harm caused by stupid hats with elastic string cutting into your chin. And I might seriously need to chill. But the silliness, the glibness, irks me. We should feed the poor, not stuff our faces with grocery-store sheet cake and icing made to freeze our arteries in a slow death by Crisco. At least, the very least, homemade pie (even from the diner) would be better than store-bought sheet cake. When I go on my anti-birthday-festivities tirade, Death by Crisco, et cetera, Tiffany nods and smiles and says,

–I see your point, yes, but you need to Chill Out.

Birthdays are number six on my list. I haven't told Tiffany or Luke about my obsession with my list, which has claimed more of my homework time. Whenever I hit a brain block in the middle of a physics problem, I find my list and add or subtract or refine an entry. When it's perfect, I might reveal the complete and polished version. Then lame birthday parties with requisite gifts and ridiculous antics will be abolished! The three of us shall proclaim to the greasy diner and its reluctant waitresses our ten (perhaps 20) commandments of adulthood. Old guys with syrup in their beards and moms with wailing brats shall be amazed at our guile. The manager will switch off the beastly vacuum to applaud.

Or maybe I will give up on the list and stick to faking it till I turn twenty-four.

At the diner to celebrate Luke's birthday:

–Luke, my friend, I hope you like it n'all.

He unwraps the long, thin package.

–Bec, it's a Bic.

And before I could read his face, he is up and around the end of the booth and smooshed up next to me. Luke is not a known smoosher. But now his arm pushes down across my shoulders in an awkward booth hug. Usually I would have been the one to rush him or Tiffany and grab with all my might. I just like the way it says so much without garbling any words at all. I am the quiet one; Luke, on the other hand, loves to talk and talk and can smoosh you with a thousand words wrapped around you like the perfect dress. Just listening to his voice makes my skin radiant and my teeth perfect white. If the media could see me glow in his spotlight, I would be a star.

–Thanks, Becca. Sign my arm?

–Sure, okay, right, sure.

I write "HB-DL" etching the letters deep across the back of his palm.

Tiffany signs his lower arm: "Kiss me I'm 17!" and "9/25/01"

Luke groans and rolls his eyes at Tiff in a good-sport kind of way. Since he broke up with Melissa last summer, Tiffany has been on a crusade to get him hooked up. The thing is, Luke is the perfect man. Not boy, man. The kid is just too good to be true, as far as I can tell. His mom passed on her dark Latina looks, and his dad gave him his respectable six-two stature. His mom gave him tight black hair and his dad gave him blue eyes. He gives himself hours in the gym lifting weights or in the school pool racking up hundreds of laps. Tiff and I take turns being the president of his fan club. He always seems to have a girlfriend. Lately, however, he gets all silent treatment when we mention so-and-so or that new girl or did you see her? He talks about World History homework or what he had for lunch or what he hopes his mom is cooking for dinner. Tiffany is undeterred.

I let it ride. Luke does not suffer from lack of love and never has. Except for the time I broke his heart. Luke and I had a thing back in middle school. I still haven't figured out why our brief romance at the end of eighth grade imploded. I know the facts—yet can't believe that it was I, Rebecca White, who played out that history. It was my fault: I got jacked up on stress about school, my parents' divorce and the way our home became Mom's house, and my obsession with getting into the yearbook. I was tricked up about junior high graduation and making it big in high school the next year. Luke happened to me when my head was in the fog of can't-wait-to-be-great in the high school world of cars and fancy-dress formal dances.

Luke and I were going out—holding hands at movies— and then I was in Florida with my mom for Christmas, where the sun, sand, and Grandma's quiet habits were a welcome world apart from the constant noise of junior high school life.

When school started up after the holidays, I hit the halls and first thing saw Luke posed against my locker, pretending not to wait for me. One hand in his pocket, the other wrapped around his stomach in a tight grip. A sick dread blossomed in my stomach. I swear that my vision glazed when I realized that not once had I thought about him over the long winter break. Inexplicable. I hated myself for it. I hadn't sent a stupid Santa Ho Ho Happy Holiday card, even. I never thought to call long-distance. I hadn't given him Grandma's address or phone number. It never occurred to me. The dread in my gut spoke loud and clear to my thick head, and I knew what it meant to be a shit. I, Rebecca, ever the oh-so-nice girl, was a total shit. He pressed a damp note into my palm and managed to strut down the hall.

The note was sweet but uncompromising. He broke up with me. I was dumped. I deserved it.

Later, when we talked face-to-face after school, he just shrugged off my horrible self.

–Becca, you're okay. Let's just be friends.

The dreaded "friends." Oh, yes.

Honestly, for real, the truth is that we have become really great, true friends ever since we broke up (he dumped me, okay?) that day in main hall. We have grown up since then. Our friendship is deep. True. Authentic. Unique, even. I owe him so much. He taught me how to pay attention to people, how to see their deep-down beauty. He saw it in me. And even when I was mean to him, even when I was a terrible girlfriend to him, he didn't abandon me. He is my heart. He taught me everything I know about love and friendship. We are friends now because we got the dating part out of the way in junior high. We "dated" as best as you can when your parents have to haul you around to the mall or to the Putt-putt mini-golf course. And we did more than just holding hands in the movies. We hooked up back before hooking up was so grossly complicated.

Kissing Luke the first time was, well, I wrote pages about it in my then soon-to-be defunct journal. I had kissed other boys before; I wasn't clueless about it. Kissing Luke for the first time was different. It was perfect. He kissed like (and looks like) a soap opera star on the rise. He had arranged the setting with an eye for lighting and mood: time alone in my basement (my mom away at some work meeting) with music and vanilla-scented candles he'd bought at the KanMart with his lawn-cutting money. He held my hand and stroked my arm for three consecutive sitcoms. Just when I was soft and ready to tell him how I felt so lost in my own head at night, he looked me in the eyes. It was the first time in my life that a boy looked me dead center in the eyes. I didn't get nervous or say something all wrong. Instead I let him look at me.

He leaned in for the kiss, and we stared into each other's eyes. I could smell breath mints. It was fine to keep our eyes open. I looked at him in the eyes. Then I let him kiss me. I felt the candlelight on my skin, and the music pulsed. I didn't even try to keep my lips plush or run my tongue along his lips like I had read in magazines at the salon. I just let him kiss me. Meanwhile, he kept his two hands pressed on my forearms. I felt like a canvas and thick hot paint was being stroked red on black on soft pink on silver across my plain white expanse.

And then, a few months later, I went away to Florida to see my grandma for Christmas break. Luke's kisses had grown less spectacular and more mechanical, less glamour and more precision. I suppose I took him and his kisses for granted, or maybe I had grown bored by our kisses. Honestly, I can't quite force into focus my memories from those long-ago sun-drenched days. I wasn't angry or hurt by Luke. I'd gone to Florida and engaged in my normal winter pastime—hours lounging in a hammock, reading Danielle Steel romance novels. Never once did I dream about Luke, the boy I was going out with, the boy I was kissing. I forgot about Luke—not in a mean way, just in the way that happens when you travel to a place far away. I didn't think about Tiffany either, but, then again, I wasn't letting her kiss me when my mom wasn't home.

After Luke and I broke up, we still kissed sometimes. Not passionate tongue lashings. Just gentle lip nestling and a bit of neck nuzzling.

I still let him kiss me, and he lets me kiss him, but we

don't cheat. So if he has a girlfriend, I respect that, and vice versa. Perhaps it's a bad habit. But it is just so nice to kiss him, innocent and soft. We have never told Tiffany about our kissing. At least, I haven't. (Maybe Luke and Tiffany hook up too and have never told me. I doubt it, but I can't be sure. I have never asked him about it. *Stop it*, I tell my inner-turmoil, mean self. *Forget such juvenile jealousies*.) We haven't kissed for a while now. I never worry about it. If I needed him, he would take me in his arms. Even if for a few minutes. That would be enough, anyways, for me, to feel right with him. To know that we are okay, no matter what.

Luke didn't have to ask any questions when I handed him his new birthday Bic.

I could have afforded something shiny that cost 50 dollars. I chose the Bic after I'd made endless lists. Who knows where we will be on his eighteenth? This may be our last birthday. I wanted my gift to be perfect. I got the Bic because, well, the thing is that I haven't told him yet about my private list, but I did write him a poem. I haven't given him that poem, but I told him about it in a moment of supreme weakness. I am proud of the poem and terrified of what he'll say about it.

I wasn't ready to share my poem, so instead I gave Luke a real poem at the diner. The coffee had long grown lukewarm and we had devoured a plate of steak fries.

I used my broken-in Bic to copy the poem in decent handwriting on a sheet of lined notebook paper.

I'm Nobody! Who are you? Are you – Nobody – Too? Then there's a pair of us! Don't tell! they'd advertise – you know! How dreary – to be – Somebody! How public – like a Frog – To tell one's name – the livelong June – To an admiring Bog!

Luke isn't into poetry and I've never been much into poetry or writing either. We have those kids at our school. They wear black and have silver barb piercings and write about video games. Or they wear pastel sweaters and khaki pants and write about Jesus and his Virgin Mother.

So, poetry was not my thing. But then one day at the end of junior year, I found this Emily Dickinson poem. I was killing time and had googled colleges and Teddy Roosevelt and blogs just to see what's out there, and one link led to another, and there I was reading her tiny poem. I copied and pasted and reduced the font infinitesimally small. I printed it out and tucked the poem in my pocket.

I memorized it. And it went 'round my head like a pop lyric. *-I'm Nobody! Who are you? -Are you—Nobody— Too?-Then there's a pair of us!* As the poem circled round inside my head, my brain buzzed. I walked with an upright swagger. Like I had this little explosive device concealed in my head that I could detonate—BAM!—in the middle of the diner or maybe during class when we slouched in our desks. Shakespeare's sonnets and even Ophelia's tragic death in iambic pentameter are all right and tight and Real Poetry—rhyme and old-fashioned English. But Emily, Ms. D, is mine, all mine. *-Don't tell! they'd advertise—you know!*

Whatever. I embarrass myself over Emily Dickinson. And this is why I try not to talk about her. And, weirdly, this is also why I had to share the poem with Luke. A force beyond my will drove me. I couldn't stop myself.

I gave him the poem at the diner on a Friday night. I got ketchup on the corner as I passed it over the tabletop.

-Luke, check out this poem.

He read it once. Then he read it out loud. Then he said,

–You tell me, Becca.

And so I told him why it rocks: being nobodies together.

–I mean, "frogs in a bog." A bog like this school, this town, you know?

He just let me go on and on, and he nodded his head and drank coffee, and then. He said,

–You should write your own poems, Bec.

His words exploded inside of me. I dove headlong into a windy tangent about Bics and how the pen is mightier than the sword and how I wondered if Emily would have used a Bic and how Bics are cheap and under-loved. I mean, a Bic is a Nobody in a bog of gel inks and rainbow-colored fine-tip markers, et cetera.

(That sentence, "You should write your own poems, Bec" was fundamental. It was divine. It was my calling. But I didn't know it then. Rebecca Before didn't know that Luke and his story would become the narrative for my attempt at writing this book, the closest I could get to a poem. The closest I can get to putting his story down.)

I mean, Luke, I am not, like, a poet, but I didn't say that out loud. I just tucked that idea inside my other pocket. Luke had this way of saying things that stuck inside me, took root, made me want to believe in my beauty, and my poetry.

When I gave him the Bic for his b-day gift—actually, two Bics tied up in a silver ribbon—he knew. But he didn't let on to Tiff. I gave him a pen; he gave me a silent affirmation of his loyalty to me. He believes in me. He believes in my capacity for poetry. He thinks I can turn fact into metaphor. This confidence in me makes me hungry for more steak fries, for the salt and sweet of potatoes and ketchup. He was Luke; I could count on him to see the Rebecca I could become. We love Tiffany, but.

Tiffany ducks down beneath the table and pops up with a box wrapped in wedding wrapping paper and tied up with a gold bow. She hoards wrapping paper and has accumulated stacks of slightly crumpled, secondhand giftwrap in her bedroom closet. When her sister got married last spring, she unwrapped every gift while the young couple packed for the honeymoon so that she could "help" her sister. She re-wraps the most important gifts using the wedding stash. Already we know that she might cry when Luke rips into her gilded gift.

Inside the box layers upon layers of tissue paper unfold. At the center, Luke finds an envelope. Inside is a 25-dollar gift certificate for Sampler's, a white tablecloth and candles steak restaurant. Luke smiles but looks at the beaming Tiffany with a raised eyebrow.

–Oh, Luke, we can all go to a real restaurant and have real food and clean water glasses, for a change.

Silence.

–I love this place you know that, but we can all go n'get dressed up, n'how about next Friday?

Luke reaches across the booth and holds Tiffany's hand in both of his for just long enough to say,

–Thank you, thank you, a lot. I mean it.

Luke doesn't meet my eyes. I do not look at Tiffany.

This is awkward. I know that Luke feels it. Tiffany looks pleased with her gift. It is a generous idea. And yet the diner was my discovery back in ninth grade after Luke and I had become just friends. I get nervous thinking about eating in a real nice place. I like the familiar diner just fine.

That is, I liked the diner just fine as Rebecca Before. I was safe and with my friends that day. Even somewhat bored with the décor and the menu. That day was seven days before Luke would call me, panic in his voice, and take me for that drive that ended in the beginning of another girl.

THE LAST SCHOOL LUNCH

The three of us hunch over our lunches. The cafeteria noise presses around us.

–What is that seething mess of sad meat you paid your parents' good money for? Tiffany asks me.

–"Cuban" sandwich, singed by our sad cooks. And, behold, the pickles. This is a grilled hot sandwich with hot pickles. Pickles are tasty. But. Grilled pickles, not so much. And what makes it "Cuban"?

Luke ignores my sandwich soliloquy and turns to Tiffany,

–Tif, how's your new boy? Where's the new boy?

–Home sick today. Just a cold.

We munch away. This was a typical day, and it felt easy to enjoy the relative calm. My sandwich lies there wide open as I build a mound of sorry, cooked pickles. Then Luke, whose shoulders were high and his voice too loud, drops a conversational bomb:

–So, I want to ask you both about something.

–Okay.

–What's up?

–A Graduation Party. I want to throw one and I was thinking that maybe we could kind of co-host it, you know? At my house? Or one of your houses? Or wherever. We should have lots of people—our families and friends, some music—maybe live? Or a deejay? And food. My mom can make the food, unless you guys would want to be in charge. And drinks?

Luke rushes on as I crush the bread onto my slab of meat-minus-pickles. I clamp my jaws around a massive bite and labor through a mouthful while Luke jabbers on about party details. I don't like this idea. Yet graduation is light-years away and there is a real chance that Luke's idea is just talk and will fall through. Before I wash down my bite with a drink of Coke, I've already concluded: Best to agree and worry about the details later. Hopefully this idea will blow over. And so I agree:

–My mom is, like, not into parties. So, like, co-hosting would be good.

–Do you think people would come to a party co-hosted by us three?

Tiffany nails it. Slams the hammer on Luke's thumb.

Nacho chips or cheese platters, whatever. But the graduation party is the Graduation Party. The graduate invites their inner circle. But since there are so many seniors, there is competition for the right people to attend your bash. It would be pathetic if we host a party and no one shows up except our parents and few weird cousins from out of town. Tiff has been invited to graduation parties ever since ninth grade. She was one of those freshmen who had connections with upperclassmen through siblings, clubs, and friend-of-a-friends. Luke went to one as a tagalong last year. He was going out with a girl whose brother graduated last year. The big brother could not object to including Luke, his little sister's boyfriend of five months. Luke dated her until the party, and then split from her the next day. Not big of him, but the party, he said, had been too much for him. His girlfriend got all: What about next year with us? And he bailed.

So, Luke wants us to throw a Graduation Party. It is a risk. It is a challenge. Luke wants to do it; otherwise he wouldn't have interrupted a perfectly bland lunch conversation with his proposition. We exchange open-faced glances, and Tiffany shrugs her shoulders. Luke clears his throat too and crams his sandwich into his face. Boys can cram sandwiches—or burritos or nachos drenched in cheese—and manage to look all the more boy-attractive. Ugh.

–Luke, let's do it, I say.

I can see the white awning of the rented tent, smell the grilled meat, hear my parents call out for me to smile and hold up my diploma.

Tiff goes,

–Okay but I have to talk to my mom n'dad, because I think that they were kinda planning to have a party at my house with my relatives n'all. So I have to check.

Luke suggests that maybe we could ask Josh or Jeff or whoever to co-host too, if we want.

–Jeff? Luke, that kid is so gay. I'm thinking he's a no.

Jeff? I think. Since when does Tiffany think he is so gay? Luke says,

–Whatever, Tiffany.

Luke said it like this: What-*Ever*, Tiff-Any. He seems super annoyed with her. He is not amused with her lack of enthusiasm, I guess. (I assume that Luke and I will gossip about her later—nothing vicious, more affectionate: just Luke and Rebecca having a good-natured laugh at Tiffany's expense.)

Luke loves a good party. I know the details will be perfect in Luke's way. People will have a great time. I can invite my mom and my dad, who have spent most of my life after age ten staying out of the same room. My mom could hang in the kitchen and fuss over the food; even learn to cook taco meat from scratch instead of using those little packets of spices. My dad could hang out in the back near the keg or the cooler or the grill, wherever he has a steady stream of liquids and a captive audience. They might even stand near each other to take their separate snapshots of Luke, Tiff, and me.

Dad is a hit with my friends. Everyone adores him (even my mother used to, way back when, I am sure). They split when I was 12, and then life got real quiet. My dad moved back to his old neighborhood. He's a decent quote unquote dead-beat dad, I have to say. He doesn't send money, because he hardly has enough for himself. My mom has worked for 20 years at Deverson & MacMillam, an assistant to the head tax lawyer. She makes enough for all of us.

Twice a month Dad picks me up for an after-school snack—French fries with extra salt dipped into chocolate milkshakes. I humor him. He is harmless, mostly. Sometimes I wish he could hold down a job for more than six months. He can sell just about anything for six months. I suspect his blowhard bosses bore him. He gets by. And he comes by to see me regular enough. He tells funny stories about his latest jobsite catastrophes. I laugh with him and decide that I will never sell furniture, cars, or insurance, ever. A few years ago he dated a girl, and things got serious, I think. He kept mentioning her for two months after she left him. She was a good woman who deserved to get out of town, he said. But.

The bell will ring in seconds and scatter us to our respective classes.

–Luke, we will make a Party List: who to invite, food, libations and stuff, music, parental duties, et cetera.

–all right, Bec. Piñata? I'm just saying.

Now we are talking. Luke loves a good piñata bashing, as do I. The baseball-bat-swinging pure aggression of it. For candy.

–Piñata, check. Number one on our list: a garish papier-mâché animal. Oh, let's make Plains High proud. It must be a Fighting Cardinal.

–genius.

–You two are terrible. (Tiffany halfway smiles as she says it.)

We laugh out loud, and Luke high-fives me. Luke laughs too loud, a strange, hysterical sound. A few kids look up from their brown-bag lunches with quizzical expressions, hoping for something to see.

Rebecca Before shrugs away his strange, hysterical laugh. She didn't know. Couldn't know. Not even a tingle. Total blindness. Total ignorance of the Luke whose pain was heat and would burn her down with the force of fully fueled jet engines. Incinerate her for the sake of his liberation. To be alive. To be a Nobody.

THIS IS THE TEST

At first he didn't tell me. Then he told me. I promised not to tell.

Luke and I sit in his mom's van. The engine ticks as it cools. We stare at our grade school. Inside the red brick walls, now so squat, we learned to write cursive. My favorite was the uppercase L. So elegant and alive with is bold loops and precise curves. It is a grownup letter. It takes up space on the page and holds meaning beneath its shadow. Love. Learn. Laugh. Lose. It is 2 a.m. I have never been out so late. I don't even have a curfew because I have never stayed out this late. I see curfews in my future.

Luke is the opposite of cool. He is a mess. All jacked up on caffeine, I hope. Red-rimmed eyes. He shoves his fists deep into the sockets. I have never seen him like this. Luke but not Luke. Cool undone. Gentleness shattered into what I will understand later to be suffering, a terrible grief. I freeze. I shake. I don't want Luke to say anything at all. I want things to be okay. I trace a cursive letter L on the seat of the car where he can't see. I want to drink coffee at the diner and use my Bic to pass notes during study hall. (I wanted to start all my sentences with I.)

    –It was a few days after my birthday. God Bec. Swear to me, swear to me you will never, never say a word to anyone. This is it, Bec. You and me.

    –I promise, no repeats.

    What should I have said? You fill in the blank.

CHAPTER TWO

TRUTH DARE PROMISE OR REPEAT

And what follows is Rebecca After. Or, rather Rebecca After Luke Tells Her about the Lake House. There will be another Rebecca. That Rebecca takes months to emerge. Rebecca alone defines that Rebecca.

Luke isn't talking to Tiffany anymore. Tiffany whined about it during lunch on Thursday.

–Where's Luke?

–Don't know. Home sick?

–No way. He is avoiding me. I saw him this morning in Main Hall.

Tiffany cracks open her Diet Coke.

–Avoiding you? Luke?

–Rebecca, darling, wake up. Luke has been all whacked out for days. He's hardly here, never comes to lunch. And when he is here, he is all: Dark and Moody.

–It's a phase, maybe. So what?

–Rebecca.

–Okay, so, yeah. I know. It's just that he's Luke, you know? Maybe he needs some space. He has his moods.

–So, what's going on with him? He must've told you something. He avoids me but talks to you. Typical. What is it?

I bat my doe eyes and bite into my sandwich. Nod and point to my mouth, raise my eyebrows, and hold up one finger. I hope to conjure some reasonable tale in the time it takes to dissolve the wad of chunky peanut butter and stale white bread on my tongue.

–Tell me the truth. Are you guys mad at me? Whatever.

–Exactly: Whatever. Really, Tiffany, there is nothing to worry about.

And then this slips out:

–It is not all about you, all the time.

Boom. A pocket of silence seals around us despite the clatter of trays, shrieks, and guttural grunts in the cafeteria. She narrows her eyes and looks at me. She doesn't like what she sees. Her alarms have sounded. She sighs louder than the thunder of trays slamming the return carts. She looks away. She chooses to play it off for now. The best defense, we both know, is to gather your ammunition while ye may. Someday, that comment will come back to get me, if and when she chooses.

The silence is thick. It's a rush of cruelty, and it makes my heart race. The thing is: Tiffany can't know the truth. I promised. No repeats.

The bubble bursts when two kids sit down at our table. Tiffany picks up her narrative thread about her latest boyfriend. My head nods to pretend that I am attentive and alert. She can talk and talk and talk. When she pauses and silence threatens to descend, I ask her, real casual:

–So, Tiff, pie this Saturday? Just the two of us if Luke

can't make it? Or bring along Stephen; that boy-toy of yours could use some pie.

Tiffany glowers in suspicion before her mad-craze for Stephen drives her past any concern about Luke. Luke is moody. Rebecca has her days of ill humor. So what? Stephen, on the other hand, is delicious.

I know she hasn't taken him for pie yet. It's an insider thing we do: We wait until we think the new boyfriend/girlfriend is ready to share with us. Then we invite them. To pass the test, they must drink the bitter coffee brew, eat both their allotted slices—whether it be banana cream, chocolate silk, or lemon meringue—and entertain us with their boothside banter. They have to exhibit at least a small measure of awe in the light of our esteemed company. If they pass the Pie Test, they become a sort of honoree at our diner gatherings. Yet they must be invited each time, and we reserve the absolute right to veto an outsider at any moment. Not that we have ever vetoed anyone. It is nice to know that we can, however.

Truth: I don't care to spend time in Stephen's company. But it makes Tiffany forget to ask about Luke. Besides, dreading pie with Stephen is ordinary, and it feels good to have something mundane to push Luke's terror a little bit deeper, where I keep it safe.

WHAT WOULD JESUS DO?

In my room. The door closed. Channel surfing.

"Bec, it was him. I am so stupid."

"fag boy"

WWJD.

WWJD.

"hunting knife"

"it was him"

Luke didn't cry when he told me, but I did. I wanted to crush up against him and hold him in my arms. Even though my arms wanted to soothe him, they refused to leave my lap at first. Finally, when I reached out for his hand, he took mine. Our hands marooned there in the space between our bucket seats. It wasn't enough. He wasn't Luke anymore. He was someone you hear about on the late news. He was a monster, a person torn up by another kid and turned into trash just like that. Now you are here, a Nobody, now you are nothing. Parents don't know about this kind of stuff. This stuff doesn't happen. I can't. Luke can't be Luke anymore.

"it was him."

Girls get attacked. You hear about it every other week in the news. Then they go away, disappear from the news. Or sometimes they are rarefied into heroes for it, turning the guy in. What Courage. What a sacrifice she made to give up her name and place herself dead center in the headlines for our dose of local gossip and gore. Girls get all serious when they are victims; they become women. Their tears anoint them and make them holy survivors. But, mostly they just go away. I don't know a single woman who has been raped. I hear about them on television. I know only girls who are about to get raped.

Boys rape. They do not get raped. Luke got raped. Luke is not a boy? "Luke is not a boy?" What does that even mean? Why does my mind insist on trying to find logic in this nightmare? It doesn't add up to anything that I can grasp no matter how I rearrange the variables.

WWJD. What Would Jesus Do? The blue plastic bracelet with the letters WWJD is on my wrist. My dad gave it to me on my sixteenth birthday. He found Jesus between weekend visits and presented me with the bracelet. After wearing it on the car ride home, I slipped into the house and found a drawer safe from my mother's discovery. Today I took it out from between folded sweaters and put it on. Now I finger my bracelet, stretching it and ringing it around and around my wrist. I trace the raised letters: W-W-J-D. My wrist and fingers are rigid as I yank it off and toss it across the room.

There is one thing I know: I am not Jesus. How am I supposed to think like Jesus? Nevertheless, I try. I have to get inside the mind of Jesus. I have to. I can't get inside Luke, anymore. I can't.

"swear"

"you can never tell a single person"

"it will kill me if you tell"

"swear"

After school, in Luke's car:

–Who was it?

–Rebecca, I don't want to tell you more. I am afraid for you too. Knowing more will eat you up, trust me. Are you fully sure you want me to say his name?

But I already knew. There is one person who could do this.

–I swear, Luke, of course. I will never tell.

–Weston.

–And the other kid?

–Roger. He must have known; they planned it. Bec?

I nod.

But he doesn't go on, he just looks at me, and I nod and don't know what questions to ask or how to make it all go away. I have his name now. I have someone to hate. My fingernails rake across my scalp, and scoops of white dandruff gather beneath my nails. My eyeballs prickle in the salt, but I hold the tears back. Tears run down the inside of my dry throat. Burning. I get out and slam the car door with all my might. I wait for him to drive off and leave me at the mall. He doesn't. He is calm.

We drive. My thoughts about rape or about Jesus scare me into silence. I want him to tell me everything, I need him to tell me more. All the details. All the incriminating evidence. (He must tell someone, and it should be me—I am his best friend, his only friend now, it seems.) We let rock music scream through the opened windows. Luke takes a corner with enough speed to squeal the tires against the asphalt, leaving a scorched trail to mark our path.

I hold my breath as the air whips my face and presses into my closed eyes. There is a magnificent chasm beneath my feet, and I hover over jagged rocks with only my own hot air to keep me afloat. My little kid self is on one side of the divide, frozen into a ponytailed statue with a sticky-faced grin. My grown-up self—a shadowy projection of all that I am now—watches me from the far side. She smiles with her eyes and just watches the scene play out, offering no words of advice. She doesn't throw me a rope.

So this is what it means to grow up.

Later that night:

My bookbag is on the floor. Unopened. Collapsing under its own weight. I feel nothing. I feel detached. At least that is something. I pick up the WWJD bracelet and tuck it between two sweaters deep in my bureau's third drawer and shut it.

ENGLISH CLASS GOES ON

Weston's life goes on as English class goes on and everything looks normal and everything feels wrong.

It is a relief to go to English class. It's a safe room, a period of fiction instead of the horror of Luke's reality.

Ms. Walters is new. This explains much. The first few months of school have taken a toll on her, however. She no longer bounds down the hall. She spends more time sitting behind her desk.

The new and the ancient teachers are the ones to avoid. Of course there is no way to avoid them. Students are assigned to teachers by counselors who lock themselves in a room with the football roster and donuts provided by the Parents Association. You get assigned. If you want to change classes, the gods have to smile. Or you have to play a key role on a varsity sport. Or be in performance choir. Or tutor grade school tykes in your spare time. Most of us take what gets dished out on our schedules with a grain of salt. You learn by the end of freshman year how to deal with the various teachers. If you don't learn, you spend a repeat year in the freshman hallway retaking Introduction to Keyboarding and or indulge in self-destructive behaviors to self-medicate. Luke rips his hangnails. Tiffany drinks Diet Coke for lunch. I pick my zits. Claw at my face until it explodes with body goo. Then hide in bed under the covers. Whatevs. But we learned to read teachers and so here we are in senior English despite all the odds.

This is English class, for high school seniors who are gone, gone, gone in their heads to college or done, done, done with high school teachers. Tiffany scored a desk within note-passing distance. Luke has Ms. Walters for English, but he has her after lunch. Thus we can supply him with the appropriate heads up for quizzes and other sundry activities to endure. The first semester of senior English we concentrate on writing our college essays. At least, a good portion of us will. Then we will glide by our second-semester term paper with research on the internet and a few pithy statistics. By the time we have finished our college applications, school will be just, well, a building. This would be fine, except we know what happens next. We have seen it happen to our older brothers and sisters. You start to moon over the bricks and mortar.

In a finely timed third-quarter maneuver, the administration will distribute weepy letters during homeroom about "giving back" and "staying connected" as alumni. We will all mock the letters. But after homeroom, on the way to art or English or lunch, it hits you: This hallway is my hallway, and next year I will be less than a ghost here. And that hurts, a bit. I am not ready to disappear from these halls. I am not ready to be a ghost.

But we are not quite there yet. It is still first quarter. We have been talking about our college applications and how we will write several practice college-application essays, but so far it is all talk. I have outlined and brainstormed and researched—okay, googled—several topics. The actual act of writing requires a jump from inertia to motion. Ms. W is supposed to act on us so that we react with equal force. She gives us the prompt: Tell about a person from history who you would like to meet. And we react: a catchy opening (maybe a quotation or startling statement, maybe a personal anecdote, but, please, not the rhetorical question unless you are desperate), a well-developed three-to-five paragraphs, and conclude without offering any new information. Ring that school bell in a triumph of academics over personal obstacles, and let it resonate. Pick me! me! me!

The historical-figure prompt can trick you up. You have to pick someone obscure enough to show that you know some history yet important enough to make you look good in his or her company. After skipping over several options, Mother Jones emerges as my subject. Easyessays.com does not have a readymade Mother Jones essay for sale. Not that I would buy it, copy-paste, change a few adjectives, insert my personalized anecdote, and wham-bam-pleased-to-attend-your-fine-liberal-arts-college thank you, madam. Whatever. At least I hadn't considered doing so before. Now Weston infiltrates every brain cell, try as I might to take Ms. Walter's lectures and free-write assignments to heart, his every move is a red flashing blip on my radar. One harmless essay bought and recycled for the college of my choice seems like an inconsequential breach of ethics. The future is not now.

I'll leave it to Ms. Walters to feel deeply about our scholastic futures. Her voice is earnest when she recounts her college experience—state school honors program, sorority, and a year abroad reading Shakespeare (and drinking pints of ale, wink nod) in England. We listen with studied inattention and assume that her passion is aimed at earning good feedback on her first-year evaluations. At least this is what we say when we gossip about her gauche black leather pumps. The gold buckle on the toe is impossibly bright and screams PayLess. Please. Or how first hour kids come armed with mints to proffer in the hopes of staving off her dread coffee-breath. (Note: Adult woman drinks coffee. See? I will learn how, I swear. But I will carry my own mints.) Or how every Tuesday she has the tuna-stuffed tomato salad from the cafeteria, which also requires students to bear spear-a-mints.

What we don't talk about is what we all notice: she is always at school, and if you catch her around 4 p.m. after her afternoon cup, she is exquisite. She is the mom you wish you had—young, hip, hot for Thoreau, but harbors esteem for Stephen King, et cetera. She knows she is a coffee-tuna dragon and thinks we owe her the mints. She is deep in love with teaching. But the most important thing about Ms. W. is that she is deep in love. She loves. Yes, it is teaching; but, it is love. She loves Emily Dickenson, Walt Whitman, and Shakespeare. Words turn her on. She has the courage to show love. Her attraction is attractive. For this we revere her. In small doses. From the privacy of our uncomfortable plastic chairs.

At least, I revere her, and I use extensive class time to consider the pros and cons of drafting a letter upon graduation to extol her pivotal role in my young life. I have been known to do this: I wrote letters to my piano teacher (whom I loved after I was allowed to quit) and to my eighth-grade biology teacher (whose flower-reproduction lecture still moves me—though I didn't mention that in the letter, of course). It is the least I could do for her.

So, this is English class. Life goes on.

Except the minute we step out of the classroom Luke's attacker waits for me behind every open locker door. He is just around every corner. He is ahead of me in the lunch line. He eats his lunch. He chugs an ice-cold Coke. I can see him from across the room. One day I am close enough to hear the rip of his knuckles as he cracks them one at a time, first across his right hand, and the then the left. And then he cracks his neck, right and left.

TAKING COUNT

Good Old Boys. One of the guys. Boys will be boys. I've heard these refrains tossed off with a shrug of the shoulders. Sometimes with a rueful smile. High school boys get rowdy and crash a car into a stoplight. What can you do? They can't help themselves. It's natural for them to let off some steam. It's the way things are. Et cetera, ad nauseam.

Weston is one of those.

Weston lives and breathes 723 steps, door-to-door, down familiar streets and past modest houses from me. We have lived in our respective houses with our respective families since our respective births. I did not always know the exact number of steps until two weeks ago.

One week ago, Luke drove me into the night and told me about true blackness. Each day since my skin thickened with acne, my neck blushed with a prickly rash. My body bristled with the effort to protect Luke and myself from the terrible knowledge that bound us together. Creeping vines twined through our veins, ready to choke our hearts. Block out the light.

I marched those steps from my house to Weston. One,

two, three . . . four hundred and ninety-seven . . . six hundred and three . . . seven hundred and twenty-three. Seven hundred and twenty-three steps, no more or less. Imagine that.

So close, so far.

I didn't ring the bell or kick the door. I jammed my fists into my pockets, and my heart raced. I am a girl, after all. I am supposed to be weak. Alluring. Charming. My smile lighting up my eyes. Well-spoken when spoken to.

A girl makes the perfect victim. A she-victim snivels and cries and worries she will be deemed used goods, a defective product despite the public outcry against her attacker. She fears that no one will ever want her, that no boy will want to kiss her after he knows her sullied history. Harboring her fears with a deep anchor, she turns her brave face into the winds. From shore she appears ready to set sail on her redeemed future. She looks like a Brave Girl. Yes, she suffers her fate with a smile for the viewing public to reassure them that there but for the grace of God. The perfect receptacle for all the guilt and fears we can't explain.

Except:

I want to slash the screen door with a butcher knife. I want to shit on his porch. I want to press the buzzer and then impale my pretty nails into Weston's hard flesh, just near the jugular pulsing beneath his soft-fleshed neck. I want a gun—a shotgun, loaded—and I want to know how to shoot like a soldier behind enemy lines. I want a huge rifle pressed into my shoulder. I want the recoil to deafen me and break my collarbone. I want my physical body to suffer the pain trapped inside my brain.

But I get scared standing there, fuming, and shaking. I

shake, embarrassed by my impotent rage. Even if Weston opened the door, I was sworn to secrecy. Promise, no repeats. I held my ground for what seemed like an eternity. Poised to fight, I didn't have the right to impose my righteous anger in Luke's defense. I let the air out of my lungs in a sad whoosh before I turned around and marched back to my porch.

One . . . ten . . . The perfect Indian summer is a gift in October. . .one hundred sixty-seven. . . Its careless beauty raised my shoe and inserted my heel through a perfectly horrible jack-o'-lantern. The face collapsed into a cavernous gape with the candle snapped in half. It's way too soon for pumpkins anyway. Halloween's eager trick-or-treaters with prepubescent candy greed in their hearts is still a month away. Even so, some little kid will discover a cruel world when they see the orange gore of their pumpkin-carving masterpiece obliterated on their very own sidewalk.

I ran the rest of the way home, my legs churned by the fuel of disgust.

Twenty-five days since Luke told me.

Thirty-three days since it happened. Jesus was crucified at the age of thirty-three. When my dad turned 33, he pointed out that he had reached the age of Jesus's death. Back then Dad seemed old at thirty-three. Now 33 seems like not enough years to live, to accomplish a life worth dying for. For 33 days Luke has been hanging up on a cross of his shame and anger, his throat constricted with the weight of his tired arms and legs. I watch from the foot of the cross. I watch him walk down Main Hall. My lips are mute. My hands are tied with the unrelenting ropes of his shame, knotted with my promise to keep Luke's secret. I wait until he rises. I wait for a miracle. One more day, then the next. I wait.

IF I CALL

We are beyond 911.
This is a nonemergency police matter.
620-225-8126.
They would trace my number.
Luke would know.

SLACK

The love of an English teacher is easily scorned as I learned on Monday during Ms. Walter's second hour English class.

Ms. Walters had given explicit instructions to arrive in class with first drafts ready for peer analysis. She had talked up college and the essays for so long, I felt as if I had already written a stellar one-of-a-kind masterpiece of sideways self-aggrandizement and had my college acceptance letter framed along with a little announcement published in the local newspaper. Alas. In my dreams, literally. And so in my fourth year of reliable on-time assignments (and perfect attendance), I joined the ranks of the slacked and ransacked losers of the back row. I was the only reputable student with no draft.

When Walters realized my failure to appear draft in hand, the air was thick with pathos real quick.

No kidding, Ms. W's heart projected straight out of her chest and hovered midair between us. She blinked. She looked at me. Really looked and then closed her eyes all dramatic and then. She shuddered.

Yes, the shudder may have been more like a muscle twitch or a tremor induced by caffeine or lack of sufficient sunlight. Whatever. It was slight, yes, okay, and it could have been a morning-after-a-bad-burrito spasm. (Not that I can fathom how she might stomach pots of teacher's-lounge coffee, tuna, *and* a massive helping of beans in one day.) Tiffany, who was there and who had her draft typed and double-spaced, later insists that I refer to the incident as "the alleged shiver."

Shudder or shiver or mirage—when I saw it, I was in deep shit by her standards. It was clear I had committed some cliché or another: the straw that broke her back, took a turn for the worse, stepped on my own shoelaces, et cetera. She returned fire with her own cliché right back at my face: I'm not beating a dead horse, or did her eyes say, I'm not beating around the bush? At any rate, she gave me a thorough three-second eye lashing. I mean, I agree that it is so obvious to "forget" one's essay—classic avoidance, classic slacker behavior. I used to hate being obvious.

She leaned in close to my face as I gathered my books before the bell and requested my presence at her desk for a moment.

In the vacuum created by 30 kids rushing toward their lockers, she told me, "Rebecca, you lost a valuable opportunity to gain feedback from your peers on your essay." I said, "I know." No apology or excuse. "I know, I know," I mumbled and almost made eye contact.

In recent weeks—since—I have learned to slack, to slide, and to ease on by with doe eyes. Her heart will heal. Ms. Walters will learn soon enough to keep her good intentions parked behind her metal dinosaur of a teacher's desk. Hearts are not an equal exchange for mints, or college essays.

Luke's draft? No chance. He didn't show up to school today. I see his ghost all day long. I feel sad stacking my books in my locker in order by subject. It used to be satisfying. The spines lined up in chronological order. Now it seems silly.

THE PRINCIPAL

Weston plans to join the military after graduation. Serve in the navy just like his dad. Serve his country. Shoot some hoops. Be a hero. Rule the school.

Weston's dad, Principal Ames, is my "pal." At least, that is how I learned how to spell *principal* versus *principle* in fourth grade. He was the basketball coach who taught social studies when I was still in grade school. He won enough basketball games to get elected head principal. I know enough about politics and the job market to know that principals are not elected, except he might as well have been. It was a popularity vote, I swear.

The one thing the students know about the principal is this: he is hard-core. He is smart and smooth. The man can wear a suit and tie. When I used to give a low whistle of approval to one of his new shirt and tie combinations, Tiffany would gag and tell me to get a life. "He is so, whatever. Focus on boys your own age. Ha."

He doesn't make small talk. He drinks coffee all day. Budget cuts are nothing but an amusing challenge. When the district cut staff, he took over study hall and after-school detention. Now kids assigned to detention run laps around the track—rain or shine—instead of doing homework. (Some kids "are afforded the opportunity" to wash his car to earn a reduction in their punitive laps.) Kids run laps for being tardy. Even kids who are exempt from gym get tricked up running laps for dress code infractions or hallway misconduct allegations. And the thing is, most kids love it. Or they have learned to keep their mouths shut.

The good thing about Principal Ames is that you can stay out of his path unless you have study hall or detention. He stays inside his office and works the phones. He is tight with the coaching staff. He eats lunch with the secretaries.

He rules the school, and the town is happy to have a respectable man in charge. They are happy to see him doing so well since the death of his loving wife when we were in seventh grade. The whole town turned out with flowers and tuna-noodle casseroles.

Her death—my first experience with funerals—was painful. A betrayal of sorts. Mrs. Ames had given me an extra slice of white cake with fudge frosting at Weston's seventh-grade party. The other kids had clustered in twos or threes with the puzzles she gave out as party favors. I didn't have a hope of clinging to any cluster in sight. Luke wasn't invited, and Tiffany had gone out of town with her family. I was alone. Mrs. Ames condemned me to my loner status by serving me a second frosted slice and then sitting next to me with her yellow skin hanging like crepe paper from her forearms. At the time, I was mortified (even though I was horribly grateful). When she died the next year, the memory of her kindness turned her death into a personal betrayal. Death was against me. We wallowed in the collective grief that gathered in the school hallways and condensed into thick, sweet milky tears on my pillowcase during the week of the viewing and the funeral. I cried for myself, against death. Yes, I cried for Weston and his dad, Principal Ames.

Mrs. Ames was in fragile health and battled cancer for all the years that I had known her. She lost her grip on life and left the principal a single father and Weston a motherless son. "Such a tragedy," people murmured. Tragedy in real life leaves an emptiness that words and gestures cannot replace. Tragedy in great works of literature begets moral courage for the survivors, as we have been taught in year after year of English class. Think Romeo and Juliet. The young lovers die so that their feuding parents can stop the mad violence. The Montagues and Capulets even commission a golden statue of Romeo and Juliet to symbolize the price they paid for their sins. Pay a price for your sins, and learn a lesson. But for what sin did Mrs. Ames pay with her life? What lesson was learned?

Ms. Walters loves that golden statue in Romeo and Juliet. (It was on the test.) Symbols choke her up and get her stabbing at the overhead with her dry erase pen. She always has us look for symbols in between the lines. Tragic, untimely deaths in literature produce lessons learned and rosy happily-ever-afters. In our school, the death of his wife made the Principal a King. We are his subjects, grades nine through twelve.

He is a man of principle too. Might is right.

His son has to live with the principal. And it seems that not all is right in that house. Weston doesn't play basketball—at least, not anymore, not since last year when he "decided to pursue other activities." I don't know what happened. But his girlfriend, Lucy, left town with her parents and never came back. Since then Weston has had a lot of time on his hands. I bet Daddy Ames makes him run laps around their house. Hard-core.

I don't know what happened, but I can guess. Weston messed up. Lucy left town. Luke, Tiffany, and I have our theories. We think she was pregnant. There is no way around it. They got into trouble. The details were impossible to discover—no one was talking. But we talked. We couldn't help but talk.

Weston holds his head up. He lifts weights. He stays in shape. He doesn't talk about Lucy. Not to the likes of us. Principal Ames shut that conversation down in their house. Case closed.

LIGHT MY FIRE

Ms. Walters is a scourge among us. Sent here by Principal Ames to lurk in our heads with her college ravings and how there will be 42 virgins in the perfectly mown quad and endless chicken nuggets with bottomless ranch dipping sauce in the multiple 24-hour campus eateries. She says college is different than high school. It is a land of novels and discussions and coffee and reasoned discourse about current events—even politics (and here she rolls her eyes in exasperation as if she can't stand to see our blank faces). Our eyes are expressionless. But we listen.

She fills us up with idealism; at least, she sees it that way. Truth: I already knew about ideals and saving the world, et cetera. We trooped into kindergarten fresh and shiny with new pencils and clean spirals smelling of the ink printed in straight wide lines ready to be filled. Second grade was a good year—the smell of glue still intoxicating. Seventh grade we survived. Then second semester sophomore year I spilled my cup of that ideals crap on some kid's basement carpet. His mom must have had a coronary when she vacuumed. Still, up until this fall when I shopped for school supplies and sweaters in shades of apple and chocolate, I wanted to be a better person, be something. The effort now seems futile. Never mind the effort to transcend my sorry state and do something that is more than just getting by today and the next day. Aren't we all bags of hot air? We are silly red balloons blown up for an hour of bliss and then forgotten after the guests have gone home—left to sag to the floor and deflate—useless—flaccid skins.

My spine curls into a deep capital C. I am *this close* to setting my cheek upon the desk and letting my eyes close despite good appearances. Still, I scrawl notes. This—what is she saying—Wife of Bath?—might be on the test, after all.

But, of course, idealism thrives here. It merges into the congested traffic on our highways of hormones and caffeinated blood. In fact, I think I squeezed out a thimbleful of thick white idealism onto my bathroom mirror last week. (That was a nasty thought; I almost smile.) By twelfth grade, however, idealism goes underground as one of "unspeakables." I am smart enough to know that I want to look dumb. I know that I know just enough about politics, art, religious ecstasy, et cetera to look dumb. So I say nothing at all about any of these things that could trick me up into looking like a "stupid teenager." We shun ideals. It hurts too much. Classic avoidance should be the theme of our school fight song. If the pom-pom girls could choreograph a half-time show. That would be rich:

Don't Go! Fight Later! Why Win?

Ms. W. goes to the football games on Fridays when one

of her students suits up, which is nearly every game. She wears the school colors, which don't flatter her. Her neck juts out of a grey turtleneck from her red-and-gold football sweatshirt. She is a rooster eager for a cackle as she stands up and joins in with gusto as the audience chants along with the cheerleaders. She is one of those adults who converted to idealism late in college; she clings to possibility and wears it like a shield against her day. Bears it aloft for us to admire. It blinds us into embarrassment (for her).

She believes that we have inner stores of moral fiber and is determined to tap into our personal wells. This is dangerous. This is playing with fire. She knows this and runs ahead full charge with a lighter ready for her easy flick of the wrist. The force of the words she chalks out for us on the blackboard chisels her wrist. She is our muse; we are her little bundles of short fuses.

Ms. Walters—just the fact of her and her shiny idealism—plants hope deep in my head: There are ideals worth the battle. Believe and don my armor. Prepare for battle. Truth. Love. Justice. Innocence. But ideals are to blame after a war is done. When we explain the carnage and the winners are white, the losers black. What starts the battle is always, always flesh. A person. Three thousand people.

Do something for Luke.

I leave her classroom armed to the teeth. As days pass, my feet grow tired from the weight of battle gear. My skin turns to a mass of sweat-induced lesions. I hide behind my latticed visor and watch. And wait. And polish my shield and sword with infinite patience born out of profound cowardice.

If Luke could tell Ms. Walters. If he could tell his mom. If he could tell. Anyone, except me.

TRUTH, DARE, PROMISE

Weston. He is the kind of kid that everyone stares at. Even when your eyes are on the teacher or you furiously take notes, your body is radar—signals bounce in his direction and then make little digital maps in your head to pinpoint his location. He doesn't say much in class. Well, he does answer questions. Teachers lob him softballs and then ratchet things up for kids who have done the assigned reading.

The truth: Weston Ames is guilty.

Principal Ames's son grew up to be a surly kid. He is on-edge nervous. Smart. Most kids tolerate him because of his father. Small-town girls salivate after him because he is the son of the principal. When he walks down the hall, most kids and some teachers avert their eyes. They don't want to see him, really. His backpack is too heavy, if you get my metaphor. You know, too much baggage, et cetera. Kids like their friends to be nondescript. Leave the beautiful to their incestuous cliques. Leave the crazies to their body-piercing pow-wows. Leave the principal's son out of the loop. It avoids conflict-of-interest issues.

Besides, he is going places and doesn't need our affections, only a due measure of adulation.

Despite the school hallway's ragged carpet, thick enough to muffle footsteps, whispers rebound off the metal lockers and magnify in your head. You can hear what is whispered about you from miles down the hall around the corner. There has got to be a physics lesson somewhere in all the high-screech frequency sound waves and refractive surfaces. Give Mr. Hilton, physics teacher extraordinaire, a few years and a brilliant insight, and he'll have the freshies out there sniffing out the story problem. This school loves hands-on learning. The thing is: Seniors don't need to math up the science of hallway acoustics. We know how it works in our bones. Years up and down this hall, years. And we know that Weston must hear all the chatter that he forges through, even when he swaggers by, throws you an ultra-smooth "what's up" with his chin, and turns the corner into the lunchroom. He plays it all cool. He rules the school.

He is in my head now, in my pants. I hear his name everywhere. This might as well be Weston Ames High School. The air smells of his cologne long after he has gone. It reeks of self-righteousness. It stinks like boy.

"Weston applied to State."

"Did you see Weston in the paper? A story about [insert blank with debate, football, feeding the homeless, rare feats of maturity for a high school senior].

"Weston asked Silvia to the movies this Friday."

"So-and-such saw Weston the other night."

"Did you hear Weston mouth off to Mrs. Craig? She cried."

Like I say, he is in my head because the whole school

is a sick, state-fair carousel spinning around him. He is the carny who pulls the switch to delight us with the whomp and turn of wooden horses. We careen mad with wonder. We wave to our parents, who have promised cotton candy after the ride. He sneers at us and gives the old jalopy gas. He makes us orbit, and, if we hang on tight and keep our smiles up, we enjoy the ride.

In yearbook class, I riffle through some old boxes as we clean out the closet. Budget cuts. The closet will be a "work room" for some teacher next year. I mind my own business. My head is a blissful, perfect blank. Then I flip open a faded yearbook, 1963: Principal Ames right there in black and white—a different man, a young man, a kid. His Homecoming date is a girl-next-door type, and smiles for the camera like they are in a toothpaste ad. His hand is on the girl's back. The electric small of her back. With the other hand he flashes a victory sign for his yearbook camera buddies. He knew that shot would get him in between the covers of the yearbook. Sure enough, after the perfect Kodak moment, he must have taken his eager-eyed little date out back to the parking lot. His juiced up hot rod under the broken streetlight and . . . Okay. Stop. This is not Weston, Jr. It is his dad. An innocent man, surely.

Dare: Can I blame him for being the father of a rapist? I do.

Promise: Weston will pay for what he has done. He will learn that what he did to Luke demands a price. He will pay that price.

Reading Comprehension:

Q. When I, Rebecca, wrote "He is in my head now, in my pants," what did I mean?

a. Rebecca is crazy in the head. Crazy how? you might ask. Support your answer with details from the text.

b. That the narrator is so messed up in the head that she has gone and on about this Weston and has forgotten to stop and smell the roses.

c. The narrator has some kind of school-inappropriate fantasy about him since he is in her pants. That is just weird.

d. I have no idea and since when is it okay to use multiple-choice questions in the middle of a story?

e. All of the above.

f. I, the reader, reserve the right to read and think what I want about Rebecca and Luke and Tiffany and Weston and Ms. Walters and Principal Ames without answering multiple-choice questions.

Promise: Weston will pay for his sin. Cross my heart.
(and hope to die.
stick a needle in my eye.
but if i may
and if i might
my heart is open
for tonight
though my lips are sealed and a promise is true.
i won't break my word to you.)

CHAPTER THREE

Rebecca Before. Do your personal best, perfect attendance, enchanted by the power of poems, Rebecca. In love with Luke and his soft kisses, Rebecca. In love with a boy who was kind to her. Then it was their senior year of high school. Luke was her best friend, more than a best friend, never less. And then you met her, Rebecca After.

Finally, let me introduce you to the Rebecca I became. She became herself on her own, Rebecca Alone. There comes a time in your life when you must choose. Your word or your life. I chose my word.

PIE INDIVISIBLE

The diner is deserted except for two booths near the entrance. Seated in one booth is a couple in their sixties. There is an atlas marked up in pen on the table. They have huge plates of eggs, bacon, and toast—the works heaped up. Their forks slice, scoop, repeat. They mumble thanks to the taciturn waitress who pours more water, more juice, refills their syrup jar.

The u-shaped corner booth spills over with six hard bodies. They are ninth graders out too late, way past their bedtimes. The kids, three guys and three girls, have Cokes and half-eaten fries scattered on plates between them. They hunch over the tabletop and yakkity-yammer away.

I steer toward a booth far across the diner where I don't have to listen to their hot-mad gossip. I turn my back on the diner and face the window, where the reflected view is bleak: I look (and feel) two-dimensional. The hair is flat, stringy. Perhaps, perhaps the split ends charged by static electricity someone might mistake for natural body. The eyes bulge and sag, the bags visible beneath all the foundation and concealer. My coral lipstick bleeds into the corners of my mouth. Though I am dead alone, I reach for a tissue to wipe it back into line. (Mom let me leave the house looking like a clown.) I stare at my eyes and contract my lids into a glare, then open wide and flatten my corneas into two mirrors. I look the same despite the distortions. I sense the manager before I see him and slide into the booth, trying to look like an ordinary girl in for her slice of pie and a bit of homework. His perky order-taking voice comforts me, oddly.

I order coffee: hazelnut cream. I order a pumpkin pie, no whipped topping. (Yes, the entire pie, please and thank you.) And water, please. No ice.

Tonight there will be no Tiffany or Stephen; there will be no Luke. Luke. Still the thought of Luke and what happened to him makes my skin crawl, my stomach rancid. I jostle to my feet and tight-ass it to the bathroom; lock the door, and dry heave into the toilet.

Questions rush in:

You didn't run? You didn't fight?

Why did you tell me?

(What did it look like? Feel like?)

I can never ask him any of these questions. I know that. It is over now, and to ask would be brutal, another attack. It would make it real. Again.

I don't have to ask Luke why Weston chose him. It is one of the unspeakables—even between the two of us.

Luke stuns girls and boys. He looks good and makes you feel like the center of the world when he listens to you. He does that to teachers, kids, even my mom. There was this kid, a new guy, a senior when we were in ninth grade. That summer he "hit on" Luke. Luke didn't know what was happening. One night he told me that this guy, Justin, called him and told him to come over and hang out. Luke had to do stuff around the house but was impressed that this senior guy called him. A few days later the guy showed up at the mall, and we had a Coke with him in the food court. Then Luke ran into him taking a walk in his neighborhood one night when the stars were out. It went on like this. They hung out by default. Luke likes just about everyone. Then one night the guy told Luke that he liked Luke, a lot. Luke told me about it the next day.

–Luke, that guy is in love with you. It's creepy.

–What? Come on—he is cool.

–What did he say exactly?

–He told me that he likes me. He likes me and thinks that we can be friends.

–Like we are "friends"?

–Becca, what?

–Luke, don't talk to him. Stay away. I mean, forget about the whole thing. He's going away, right, to KU?

Luke stayed away. He invented excuses when Justin called, didn't call back. Then Luke went away with his family to a camping trip in Colorado. When he got back, Justin was long gone to college. Justin emailed sometimes and even wrote Luke chatty letters about his classes and the bars. But I told Luke, never write that kid back.

It was a just a summer blip, a surreal side trip into a murky world where we didn't know the rules until. Until Tiffany asked,

–Whatever happened with that Justin kid?

It was at lunch during the first week of sophomore year and her crafted casual tone set off all kinds of warning bells. My jaw stopped mid-bite into my pb & j. Luke stammered that he heard from so-and-such that Justin had left for college, not sure where (followed by a carefully indifferent shrug).

Tiffany had heard some stuff about him, that he was (she lowers her voice),

–a fag, you know? Justin tried to hook up with that kid, Matthew Rutgers. A bunch of guys kicked their asses at the end-of-summer bonfire at the lake.

She had heard about it from Stephanie, a senior in her ceramics class.

–Matthew is a fag, as it turns out. Now he's all "out n'proud" and runs some gay-support club for teens at the Y. Parents are freaked. But that Justin kid, well, I just wanted to know what everyone says about him.

Weston was at that party. It was his lake house. Maybe he saw the fight. He must have known the rumors about Justin. About Luke.

I've been in the locked bathroom for a long time. The manager knocks and asks if I am okay, do I want a to-go box for the pie? I open the door and teeth-smile and deliver a big "No thanks!" He raises an eyebrow, shrugs, and walks back to the vacuum. Slumped into the booth, I serve myself a small slice—razor thin. For the next hour or so, in between an attempt at homework, I eat my way through the entire pie, one slice at a time, one putrid pumpkin bite after the next. Thanksgiving season.

Nothing happened between Justin and Luke—at least nothing like kissing or hot-touching or feeling-up. (Shudder.) Luke would have told me. Yet kids at school know that Justin had called up Luke, they had hung around. Apparently, this was evidence enough to make Luke one of *them*. Nothing happened between Luke and Justin, but I don't have to guess why Weston chose Luke.

Weston called Luke and asked him to hang out, at the

lake house; and Luke went.

Luke wanted to go. He wanted Weston's social seal of approval.

Luke went there, happily. He knew Weston was a jerk. But Luke went.

The deadweight in my stomach—all that sugar and squash and flour and Crisco—stays put. No more vomit. The hazelnut coffee is cold and stale, tasteless after all. My hands twitch. I finish the entire pot of coffee. My heart hurts erratically.

THE PEN IS

Sunday evening Luke calls from a pay phone in the park downtown. His voice is hollow and the sound of the winter winds tinge my own lips blue as I press my ear into the phone and nod into the hallway mirror. He is frantic.

–Bec, did you finish your homework?

I tell him yes. He says nothing. So I rush on,

–Ms. W gave us a list of vocabulary words to memorize. I researched holiday traditions—Christian/Jewish/African-American/and permutations thereof—for my next journalism deadline. I downloaded articles and printed them off, but my ink cartridge crapped out. Half of the pages have a blank strip down the middle. I tried.

Luke gets on my case. He cares about me. About me getting my work done.

–Go out and get a new cartridge, Bec. The store is open 'til midnight, I think. Get information about Mexican traditions, the foods, and get someone to check your Spanish—you are hopeless, I mean tragic with your accents. Why are accents so shitty for people? It pisses me off to see how crazy-stupid people write Spanish.

Turning from the walnut-framed mirror, I press my spine into the wall. The faster Luke talks, the harder the goose bumps. I step across the hall and lock the bathroom door, leave the light off. It is better in here: dark, clean, a locked door.

He shouts through the cold winds ripping at the phone and says he'll call back.

I punch the phone off and set it on the toilet lid. I kneel there, next to the little altar I have made. The white ceramic bowl with plastic yellow roses on the tank. The phone ready to spring to life on the lid. I lower my forehead to the cold tile floor, curl into a fetal position on the bath mat, breathing in its mustiness.

11:34 p.m. that night the phone rings again. It is Luke, of course. I was wide awake in bed with the phone in my palm, my finger trigger-happy on the talk button.

–Luke.

–Yeah, it's me, Bec. You weren't sleeping, right? I'm freezing my bejeezits off in the park. Listen. I was thinking, hey, remember when we first met?

Of course I do. I sit up in bed and turn on the lamp. My spiral notebook is bedside, my Bic nestled in its spine. Luke spills out the story as if I didn't know it, hadn't told it over and over until it became a legend, our myth.

–It was at the start of seventh grade. When you sat at the lunch table with us, I thought you were one crazy tomboy girl. You were—we were—such scrawny shits. Rob sucked in his big gulps of milk and air and belched like the pig he still is. He was the king of gross, until . . .

The pen slides out of the metal coil and I uncap it.

It is clear to me that Luke has to tell it; I have to listen.

–until you piped up: Come on–that is so elementary-school stuff! And then: I can do better than Rob!

Luke laughs, I swear he slaps his thigh and slices his face with the biggest grin. I nod into the empty bedroom. I take my Bic and trace its thick blue ink over the sea-blue veins just below the surface of my wrist.

Flex. Trace. Turn. Trace.

–and you drank all your milk in one long shot. That milk always stank! I swear you did that just to be a drama queen, and then you looked Rob in the eye and Let. It. Rip.

He laughs good and long.

–and I knew,

I supply a verbal nod:

–You knew.

–I knew right then you were some kind of girl. The look on Rob's face was so royal-red. That kid was shown up by a girl, a skinny redhead at that. I had Rob last year in English, yeah.

–Luke.

He circles back and tells the story afresh, this version has superfluous details added in about the food (chicken 'n' noodles, peas, and those hot white tubes of bread loaded with government butter, dripping in it) and the other kids (Christopher and Tom) and then about gym class with Amy Silverton farting during the Presidential Fitness test, et cetera. He raves on through the history of us, working his way toward the here and now.

I stop nodding. Instead I concentrate on my wrist, finish the pattern of ink on the left and switch to the right. The pen is awkward in my left hand; so I nudge it deeper and watch the ballpoint make a channel in my pliant skin. Luke's voice throbs into my ear and I keep at it, my personal tattoo, until blood rubs raw into the ink. Trickle drops. My blood runs blue. Flex. Trace. Penetrate. Bleed.

My spilled blood doesn't shock me; the pain is the most hysterical thing I have seen for weeks. It makes me want to laugh.

My laugh matches Luke's. My flat doe-eyes point straight into my dark vanity mirror.

–You're killing me, Luke, really. It's too funny.

The next morning, I turn off my alarm right away. No snooze. I stay in bed. I stay home from school. I am sick. My arms hurt. Mom feels my forehead and tut-tuts and believes her daughter's fever. She tells me to drink plenty of hot mint tea, heat up some canned soup, and call her at the office if I need anything.

THE ADMIRING BOG

Sophomore year Tiffany begged me to go along with her to Jason's party. She needed me for the company, someone to walk in with, and someone to blame when she wanted to leave. Tiffany can rely on me to play my part. And if she didn't drag me along, I would never have the courage to go. We arrive to the house. I am ready to escape before we even step into the backyard or inside the barn or down into the rec room. That night I watched us at the party, both there and outside my body at the same time. In the moment and watching the events unfold from a corner of my brain. It ended with us parked in front of her house. Watching the sprinklers.

There is always the one spigot gone awry that fails to explode. Water pools near its off-kilter base; water sucks the lawn down into a rotted vortex of over indulgence. Too much water can kill just as surely as not enough. Too much water. Too much party.

I wonder if I should tell Tiffany's dad about the broken valve. His lawn may suffer, but it's not my business. He probably knows and doesn't need to hear it from me,

Tiffany's high school friend whose house has a "lawn" where poison ivy and dandelions are allowed to flourish. My dad never did pride himself on a carpet of grass thick enough to balance a wineglass. Benign neglect has done wonders for our patch of earth.

I think of that broken valve and its gurgling spring even though it has been two years since Tiffany and I sat parked in my mother's car in front of her house at 3 a.m. Our parents knew we had been at Jason's house—Jason, he of the mother who volunteers to read to elementary school children and of the father who works for the city. Tiffany's lawn was a dark emerald that smelled freshly cut as it always did no matter the time of day you strolled by to admire their rose arbor in summer bloom.

The secret: lots of water. Copious rivers of H_2O.

Jason's party was a mix of people—seniors and freshman and everything in between, including those graduates who float around town in part time jobs and a mist of abandonment. They come to these parties and take over the corner keg with gossip trashed out from both sides of their mouth. Each party after their graduation they lose a layer of mystique. That particular party was sophomore year on the last weekend of spring break. School would start up on Monday, along with the push toward prom and then graduation.

Tiffany drank that night for the first time. She took a beer from Jason, the good host, and fingered the plastic lip with her tiger-pink manicure. I had watched the Thai lady at the mall labor over those nails that afternoon. Now the hard-pink shells accentuated Tiffany's laughter as she traced the cup's mouth in slow, deliberate half-circles. She didn't put it to her lips at first. She was worried about her lipstick. Plus, I knew she hated the smell of beer. She wouldn't want to drink and have her ineptitude displayed by a grimace. I watched her listen and nod to the cluster around the keg. When she turned away, to look for me, she dipped her head and sipped. Her eyes came up out of that plastic cup already bloodshot from the effort—the manicure, the outfit, the entrance, and now the introductions. It was going to be a long night.

I settled into a couch with a few girls I knew from freshman biology. The last time I had seen them, we'd been slicing frogs. We used our scalpels with dexterity; our plastic safety glasses in place. Never once did I feel sorry for the ugly frogs. Salmon and cows—all farmed these days to be grilled up and slathered with butter or pressed in between soft white buns. Those frogs must have been farmed. They never had a real life. Never croaked for a lover from the wet ditches on a hot summer night. They didn't swim in black hordes losing soft whisper tails. They didn't grow lungs or sprout legs. The frogs in biology were dead long before they got to our labs. They had never seen a bog.

I used to daydream about my dissection frog from the time I had tucked her into a plastic dish until we met again in the next lab. I imagined she has been created in a test tube. One frog egg nestled in some nutritive base. A battalion of frog sperm injected by hypodermic. One sperm nestled into one egg and the rest left to die somewhere off in the agar. That one frog, my frog, (I wanted to name her Eliza, but Tiff said that was just too sad, to name her and see her cut up, her tiny legs pinned down) sprung fully formed from the egg and its sperm. Grown under the harsh lights in a laboratory. Without true summer air ever deep in her lungs, my pristine Eliza was put to sleep and another dose of chemicals turned her perfect innards into a museum for me to slice and poke and learn about the natural world.

My former lab partners—Jennifer and Ashley and their cohorts—did not want to talk about frog hearts and livers that night. They too had plastic glasses filled almost to the tops with beer. A survey of the room gives away the secret to fitting into the scene.

The secret: Copious amounts of beer.

We sat back into the deep cushions and observed the masses milling here and there, back and forth. We made small talk about what we had done over Spring Break. TV. Sleep. Work at the mall, et cetera. I didn't tell them about the fight with my mom. Normally, no one ventures the traumas of being at home too much with parents and brothers and sisters they realize they hardly know and, worse, hardly care to know.

Party = light and bright topics.

My hair twirled around my finger; I noticed myself twisting it this way and that. It was a reflex in response to so much hair flicking, neck touching, and other nervous habits: a side part changes from left to right as a hand rakes through long straight oceans of blonde locks; a section of hair near the eyes left loose from a barrette gets tucked, then re-tucked behind an ear; red fingernails traced a hard collarbone arched out of V-necked T-shirts. One girl had her right hand on her hip, on the gap between her jeans and her shirt, where her bone tented the electric-tanned flesh. She rubbed the articulate bone each time she sipped her beer. The gesture was seductive to all the girls in the room, who memorized it.

Tiffany perched on the edge of a barstool and set her glass on the table next to her within reach. She played with the rim as she gossiped with the boys. They talked about baseball and then about music and back to baseball. It was rough, their talk. Bursts and gulps of sound. The drink pulled up the stage curtain and got them a bit high on conversation that climaxed with joke telling. Filth. But. Hilarious. Wife beating, jacking off, racist jokes. We hear those jokes in comedy shows on cable. A certain breed of boy studies those shows and then spreads the humor at first one party, then the next. I see Tiffany blush—whether it is from the jokes, the beer, the tightness in the room, or a rush of chemicals inside her head, I can't say. People come and go. Then Tiffany is gone.

I came with Tiffany. I was in charge. The other froggers watch me go and wish me luck finding her. I look in the living room, up the stairs in the guest bathroom (potpourri petals spilled across the vanity and linoleum). She is nowhere.

She is outside. A few kids have escaped the dank and yeast of the basement for a blanket on the lawn under the stars. Mike was there and Weston. The others I don't remember. Mike slurred at me, "Sit down, M'lady," and made wide circular gestures to draw me closer.

It was late and I needed to get my mom's car back, not to mention it wasn't an ideal time to piss off my mom any further. But. The moon. Spring in the air. Tiffany's voice inside my head, amplified by her pleading eyes, –Relax, Rebecca.

Tiffany and I settled into each other, my hands behind me to balance her weight pressed into my upraised knees. For the first time that night, I began to breathe. The talk here was fast and bursty. Pitching. Homeruns. St. Louis Cardinals. Steroids. KC Royals. Homeruns. Red Sox Nation. Et cetera. The boys' voices soothed me. No landmines here, just boys talking baseball on a lawn under the stars. Tiffany rocked right and left on my knees to find a nook between my kneecaps for her curved spine.

–What about you, Rebecca? Do you play ball?

Of course I played softball. Everyone knew that I played first base for a tournament team in the summers. But when Mike said, "Do you play ball?" he slid into the word *ball* and cocked his eyebrow. We all laughed. Mike was a senior. I smirked at him and then caught his eye across the blanket and played it coy (even though my heart had seized):

–Mike? Do you play ball? I mean, how often do you practice ball?

Weston chimed in:

–What's your RBI average, man?

Mike rolled over in tears. I laughed at him, laughing at me.

Weston caught my eye and grinned. (My cardiac valve seized, the blood gurgled inside my chest.) He didn't say much after that, and didn't talk to me.

That was sophomore year. Weston's girlfriend, Lucy, sat behind him, her legs a perfect circle around his waist. She propped herself up, like me, on her arms and hooked her bare feet around Weston. He had one hand on a beer bottle, the other gripped her ankle. Sometimes she leaned forward and wrapped her arms around his neck, her head tucked between his head and shoulder. She clung to him.

Lucy didn't say much, but when she did it was like thunder. She had opinions, that girl, about just about everyone and everything. One time at lunch she told off a girl for "cutting" in line. She didn't have much to say about baseball that night. She was subdued, smiled and drank beers. Tiffany brought her a fresh one. Not too much later she got me to make a keg run too. The blanket was only so big, and when a new batch of girls emerged from the house, Tiffany and I got the hint. The rest of the night I spent at my post in the basement, my tired legs draped over the soft leather couch until Tiffany was ready to go.

We stayed too late. I drove back to Tiffany's and we just sat in front of her house. We were already so late, it didn't matter anymore. Besides, we knew that her parents could see us parked in front of the house. They could relax knowing that I had taken her home.

–Bec, can you believe how much I spent on these stupid nails and this one's all busted? It will take me all day tomorrow to get them looking decent.

–Maybe you should go back to the mall and complain.

–What's the point?

–You paid a lot.

–Bec, there is no way I could have gone alone tonight.

–Seniors all over that party.

–Next year, we'll have the parties.

–And the next year, we will be the Seniors. Seniors!

–This year's Freshmen look like babies.

–Clueless and so cute.

–Weston is so cute, isn't he? I can't believe *we* hung out with *him*. And Lucy is so funny. And I love how Lucy and Weston are so in love. Did you see how she was all wrapped around him and how she had her head nestled on his shoulder? So sweet.

–She is so bitchy-in-a-good-way, you know. Smart, I

heard.

–Yeah. And Weston has such amazing eyes.

The sprinklers clicked and whirred to life. Shit. The time. Tiffany told me not to worry about curfew because she knew her mom trusted me. She knew my mom trusted her. Besides, the party was harmless. Jason's parents had been home the entire time. I sat and watched the sprinklers while she jabbered on. It was then that I heard it: the silence of frogs. The lawn was brilliant and lush, water teamed up from the earth, except there were no frogs singing here. This side of town had a different breed of bogs.

Tiffany and I have been in the bog together for years. The bog is still the bog. But now I understand that Tiffany is a Somebody in the bog. She knew how to act at the party sophomore year. She played their game. I sat in the basement, trying to blend into the wall of music and talk about frog dissection. When I made small talk with Mike and Weston, my heart was dead tissue and my armpits emitted formaldehyde.

We are the seniors now. I'm Nobody, which is fine with me. Tiffany is not a Nobody. If she knew, she might croak Luke's secret to the admiring bog. She wouldn't tell to be malicious. She would be trying to help him. But in this town's bog, secrets rot.

I need Tiffany to be Tiffany, to stay that girl I cradled on my knees in the ripe spring air. I want her to be on a blanket with boys talking about baseball. I want to take her to the mall for a manicure and listen to her consider colleges. I want her to know Luke as Luke, our Luke. I can't tell her about Weston.

CARTRIDGES

From deep beneath my warm, soft, down comforter, I rationalize that skipping school today (for the third time) is for a worthy cause: my college-application essay. It must be finished before Christmas. In a few weeks we'll drive to Florida to see Grandma. There I can delude myself that the world will revert to normalcy, back to the way it was before I had to constantly work to not think about what is right, what I should do, and what I can do. I used to think that I would give my life for a friend, but that was before life taught me that sometimes friendship costs even more than your life.

After Mom leaves instructions to drink mint tea with honey and to call her at lunchtime, I force myself to stay in bed for 15 minutes and listen to the walls. Maybe I do have a fever. My head hurts, and I am bone exhausted. A long hot shower, followed by a bubble bath, fades most of the ink from my wrists. Stupid. Rubbing alcohol dabbed on my arms helps to remove the ink, and then I smother the trace wounds with antibiotic cream. I wrap an Ace bandage around the worst of it and don a thermal T-shirt under a turtleneck. It is good to be swaddled.

Tea. The computer.

I type in *great historical figure* and the links lead me to Alexander the Great, Abraham Lincoln, and Sigmund Freud before I get sidetracked at a site that details the slaughter of innocent chickens, gentle cows. I reconsider becoming a vegetarian, but admit that my carnal desire for homemade chicken 'n' noodles and a good Salisbury steak dominate any latent herbivorous tendencies. Google: *carnal.* The images are gruesome. I close my eyes to avoid the pixilated-perfect dense curves and pubic black forests.

Google: *historical great american woman.* I skim pages and lick my dry lips each time I see something worth bookmarking. Please, please let me find a great historical woman whose life story can inspire me enough to pound out my college-application essay.

Then, without much thought, I google: *boy rape.* I scroll down the first several pages of links: prison, hate, priest, incest, hate, boys, hate, healing, et cetera and including:

Boy Rape - Rape Story, Date Rape. Looking for Boy Rape (PHOTOS, LIVE-ACTION MOVIES AND REAL STORIES)? It's all right here! www.libertyforyour nightsanddays.com.theme3/article89/.

Here it is. Men get rich off boy rape. I sit transfixed, more naked than the flesh splayed out across the screen in hard little bodies, tiny erect penises. And I haven't even entered a credit card number.

My blood freezes in my veins. Then explodes into vengeance—running hot, fast with desire. Do something. My voice inside my head, *Do something, Rebecca.*

Inertia to action. Equal and opposite reaction. My reactionary gene clicks on. Off/On. On. I didn't know I had that button.

I yank on my boots. Grab the keys, my lipstick. I forget my coat. Drive in a mad-craze to the computer store. It turns out that Luke was right about the ink cartridges. He chastised me for being lazy when I told him I didn't print my homework for lack of ink. Luke was right. I will need some ink. Not for homework and not for my college essay. I need to print off some of these websites. I need to see them in black and white. I need to gather evidence.

The bright, box store is empty at this time of day. I try to look busy as I search the aisles. I bully the sales person to hurry and ring up the stuff. Perhaps he thinks I am late for an appointment or my boss needs those cartridges now, now. I dread explaining why I am not in school. But no one asks. The bored guy smiles and asks me if I found what I was looking for. I say, Yes, thank you, and watch him ring up the two cartridges. I also get a hanging file box with a lid and a cheap metal key.

My heart skip-beats all the way home:

> promise-truth,
> no-repeat,
> truth-promise,
> no-repeat—
> dare.

The college essay can wait. Ms. Walters will give me a zero for the assignment. Okay. Okay. I am eager—I feel alive—and impatient with red lights and minivans. I want to get home and read, learn, understand, find a way through, find a way out. Research first, then find my way.

UNSCHOOLING

The morning I wandered into the world of internet gore, I found porn or self-help support groups—the former required a credit card and the latter a password. With my hair tied back and my feet in wooly socks, I concocted usernames and passwords and researched the terrible truth of boys and rape. In regular 15-minute intervals I broke the silence with loud knuckle cracks, my neck popped in a chain of firecracker explosions. Late that night I crawled into bed knowing more, but feeling less and less. Numbness took over and I fell into a fitful sleep, dreaming of a test that I had forgotten to study for, my notes lost in a locked car. Ms. Walters had a rash spoiling her lovely hands.

This morning I reach for the water faucet and ask the crucial question: Shall I skip school (yet again)? The answer comes to me as I rub dry my right leg, rough with stubble: Do not stay home (again), go to school, and then ditch. It was crystal clear: Lunch time. Head toward the hot-food line, and then keep going out the side door. I have a car. I have gas. I have a library card. The 'brare has free internet access, and I have the passwords tucked away in my brain.

At lunch I hit the cold metal handle of the side door with all the confidence I can muster and walk out with my head held high. Of course, I have to skip English, and Ms. W. will mark me absent. The office will check attendance and let her know. If I am lucky, she will have a million other things on her mind and chalk it up to administrative error. After all, I am just not the type to stroll out of school midday.

It feels brilliant. The sun in my face as I exit the school.

The library's middle-of-the-afternoon on-a-work-day crazies lumber around the shelves and shift in the ratty chairs. I spend almost 30 minutes at the ancient computer terminal searching titles and jotting down call numbers. An old guy, stubbled and reeking of day-old cigarettes, reaches out to help me pick up my backpack as I gather my things to stand. I hoist it up and away from him, escaping into the stacks with a grimace. He stinks and has nothing better to do than hang around and help 17-year-old damsels in distress in the library?

It's creepy how you can go along in life and never know a thing exists. It humbles me and excites me at the same time. There is so much out there to learn once the right questions make you need to know more. For years a certain topic is not inside your head at all. Then you seek out a title or two in the search catalog. You walk your empty head over to locate the stacks with the call numbers you may have walked past a hundred times, and there right before your blind eyes: 50 books from every angle on a subject you would have sworn didn't exist. In fact, the subject did not exist. Then, it does. Poof. People—real live human beings who eat pie and drive sensible cars and pay bills—researched and spent huge amounts of time fixing my problem before I even knew it was going to be my problem. I start from the upper left-hand corner and scan the rows. Each time a title seems vaguely useful, I yank it into a pile. I stagger under the volumes and then dump them across a large oaken table near the restroom and in sight of the reference librarian.

This is what I catch in bits as I skim the chapters, looking for Luke: people rape and get raped. Boys rape. Boys get raped. Criminals get raped in prison all the time. (I've seen that played out in TV crime dramas. There is always the joke about bending over in the prison shower.) Priests abuse, molest, assault boys. I've heard that too in the news, but these books have real stories. I hold these stories in my hands and turn the pages, going deeper into the darkness. Boys tell in their own words how it happens. The details make me cringe; yet I can't tear my eyes away.

One story has a grown man recounting his abuse. He was ten years old, a difficult child whose parents left him at the Christian summer camp grateful to have him off their hands for the summer. They imagined him singing Christian songs around the campfire after a day of archery and fishing. He did love the arrows slicing through the summer sun and piercing the targets with a satisfying sound. It was the nights that would haunt him the rest of his life. After darkness fell and the cicadas started their relentless buzzing, the pastor couldn't help himself. "You are my darling, he whispered over and over as he got inside my sleeping bag, the other boys asleep, and I tried to keep my legs tight together but he tore me up inside." The pastor took perverted care of him. The boy didn't tell a soul until his pain consumed him years and years later. By then the pastor was dead. When I put down the book, the word *darling* lodges in my head. I put down the book. I can't put down the word, darling. The pastor used it to trap a little boy inside a sleeping bag. It's a word my mother used to say to me when I pleased her and made her proud.

These books are filled with mothers who suck off their little boys. Words I know: *Mother, suck off, little boys.* I read the sentence: *Mothers suck off their own little boys.* I don't want to let the subject and the verb and the direct object add up. The words on the page come alive with the force of a memory. Now that little boy, his mother, live in me. I don't need any guests to complicate the tea party in my brain right now. But there they are, not caught in the act, thankfully, but worse: holding hands and weeping silent tears behind my eyes.

My mom is an angel. My dad an icon of nonaggression. There is not a perverted uncle or grandparent in my family. At least, none have touched me, yet.

I check out ten books. A crumpled old suit with a pronounced limp grins through bad breath and offers to help out a young lady. No thanks. I put the books in my trunk and arrive home precisely at 3:45 (my usual after-school arrival).

I do not stack the books on my shelf. I do not put them under my bed, hidden behind the comforter's deep folds. I do not put them in my closet. I do not put them in the basement. I find a spot in the attic near the one bare bulb my mom installed there all by herself after Dad moved out. It is winter up there and my mom hates the cold.

Darling

Now that, *darling*, is tricked up. Like, with a capital T. Tricked up.

SILK

Still no college essay, as you might have guessed.

Ms. Walters's head explodes with exasperation at my indifference to my collegiate future. But. The future does not exist for me anymore. I am caught in a spider web. My limbs encased in deceptively delicate silk. My extremities have lost their skin, my bones sing with the wind that whistles where the marrow used to be.

My doe-eyes, bright and startled in the incandescent school lights, reflect Ms. Walters's spent emotions. And blink.

She grants me an extension.

She knows that I spend too much time writing for the school newspaper. This is the last straw. I had better shape up, get my act together, work in my own best interests, and do my personal best. Et cetera. And so forth.

I promise my personal best. She is frustrated with me. I know she cares about me. Not the essay. I look at her and all I can manage is to hold her gaze and blink back tears. I turn away. Pick up my stuff and mumble promises on my way out.

MORE THAN A FEELING

Luke called after school on Thursday. I was sitting at the kitchen table, drinking a glass of two percent. My homework was piled in neat stacks: English, physics, and history. I was trying to do my personal best. I come home. I do my homework before I allow myself to do anything else. No TV. I don't enter my bedroom. My pillows sing gentle lullabies if I crack the door. I don't call anyone. I sit in the kitchen, drink my mint tea or water or milk, and stack my spirals. I arrange my Bics, two-by-two.

Luke calls. I answer the phone.

He comes over, and I answer the door. I hug him, but he twitches and twines away from my arms to duck inside the house. We don't go to the kitchen. I know he can't sit still to fake watch TV. When I open my bedroom door, the goose-down comforter invites us with its feathery burden of cool linen and acres of lightness. Luke loves the comforter—has always loved to wrap up in it when we watch movies or stay up late just talking, eating popcorn. He flops on the bed and rolls over, pulling the comforter across his chest. His tennis shoes and his tight curls are visible. I sit on the edge of the bed. Soon my eyelids ache with dreams, with forgetfulness. With Luke.

–Skooch over.

He rolls toward the wall, keeps his face there. His broad shoulders standing on edge are mountainous. The Great Divide. I slip off my boots and pull an afghan from the end of the bed over me. I lay down my spine, one vertebral click at a time, flat on my back. I press the afghan across my chest and put my arms down on top hospital style. Nurse! Bring us the memory extractor and some high-dose codeine (liquid form, grape flavored).

Yet so much would be lost. I am not ready to give up my Luke memories. He came here today. He knew that he could. He knew that I would be doing my homework. He knew that I would answer the phone for him. He knows that I always answer the phone now, just in case.

We sleep a solid, hard 45 minutes.

I wake when Luke thrashes his legs from the comforter. When he tosses it across my chest, waves of heat rise to my face. He says,

–Let's go for a drive.

–Okay.

–Let's just head out down Fifty-sixth.

It is the road toward the sand hill dunes, where the prairie grasses meet the cottonwoods in a groundswell of muted golds and winter-bark blacks. Tiffany lives in that neighborhood.

Luke drives my car. He pops in some Van Halen and cranks the volume. We pass the last suburban ranch house. I sit back, my head fuzzy from the nap, my mouth gamey. I look for gum in the glove compartment, but no such luck. We drive past a fenced pasture with horses trotting toward us. I check my seatbelt and run my hand between the waist restraint and my jeans. I check my reflection in the visor mirror: sleep marks and eyes bejeweled by the late afternoon light. I am okay, I see. I put the visor back into place and plant my two feet solid on the floor mat. I want to laugh. The land flattens the road a straight arrow toward the retreating horizon.

I crank up the heat to max. I roll down my window and lean my chair back. I put my hands over my eyes. I fly. Free Bird.

Luke isn't talking.

Landscape rolls by, and I stare at the gnarled trees, the winter-worn yuccas and scrabbled grasses, gold-rotted by the dry winter. I have seen this all before. But not at dusk with Luke cruising along with the guitar riffs deep in Lynyrd Skynyrd, the air screaming through my hair, the strands like feathers working against gravity.

I don't say anything. In fact, words seep out of my head. Electric guitar fills the vacuum.

Luke puts his seat back and drapes an arm over the wheel. The asphalt is razor, the light slant, and the air crisp.

He slows things down. We cruise the prairie at 50 miles per hour. The heater blasts. My eyes are closed again, and warmth spreads from just beneath my collarbones. My hipbones rub little fires, sending smoke into my thighs. My shoulder presses into the seatbelt. There will be an angry red welt there tomorrow.

When I open my eyes to look at him, he gauges my mood in a glance. He turns back to the road, the muscles around his eyes soft. He laughs. And I join him. He snaps off the music. The wind fills the car, and the road takes us. It's more than a feeling, more than a feeling.

Luke drives into the golf course. We turn the music down low, roll up the windows. Houses rim the dead fairways. Soap opera scenes play in their oversized front windows: men and women rise for an extra napkin, shift in their seats to reach the mashed potatoes. We stare into the windows, crawl along in the car. We trace a course along the holes. He stops, we tumble out, and quietly close the doors.

I run, close to ground, thriller-movie style, to the center of a deserted putting green. He follows. We collapse, air sucking. Hot from the car, the winter chill doesn't invade us.

We collapse onto the ground and catch our collective breath.

Even though I want to ask him questions, I stay silent. I hold back because I don't want to hear the answers, now. Now I pull the winter stars down into my throat and let the white-hot distance hum inside me.

I know that he will talk about it when he can. Luke—this Luke, on the road and spying on the golf crowd—is at work behind his gaunt high cheekbones, shifting through the pages of his story. He will tell me, when he knows how the story begins—or how it ends. But it has to make sense for him. He has to tell me how it happened. Then he will make sense to him, finally.

The word *darling* comes to mind. It makes me sad-sick: that word used to mean goodness and gentle touches. Now it means betrayal. I want to touch him, be touched by him. If only I could stroke his head, smoothing away the worry creases on his forehead. If only I could tell him about the other boys in the library books who have known the evil he can name.

My eyes shut against the mad-distant stars, I hold this truth: Darling, you are my darling Luke, and you, here and now, this matters—we mean something right here and now.

•

DAD

The French fries are soggy today and need salt. Dad and I debate ten minutes before ordering a fresh batch. The fry is a delicacy, especially when eaten dunked in chocolate milkshake. We hate to ruin a visit with substandard potatoes.

The new batch sears the top of my mouth with hot oil, cauterized with a shower of salt crystals, and cooled by a prolonged suck-down of milkshake. Dad talks about his new job. I luxuriate in my oily-salty-sweaty, after-school snack.

While dad talks my mind suddenly pulls up the summer he took me to see the Kansas City Royals play the St. Louis Cardinals. It was before my parents split, and I had just finished fourth grade. He'd loaded the car while my mom hovered over my attempts to pack my backpack. It was a long drive to the stadium, and we planned to spend the night in a hotel outside of Kansas City after the game. I labored over my choices, bringing both the jeans and the shorts (two pairs of each) to prepare for any kind of weather. Mom pressed a ten-dollar bill in my hand for cotton candy or peanuts at the ballpark.

The wide highways ran smooth toward Kansas City. I listened to my headphones or read or did word puzzles with my dad. He supplied nouns, adverbs, and verbs for endless games of Mad Libs. When we stopped the games, he turned up talk radio and I watched out the window.

The Royals won, but I don't remember the final score or even who pitched. The thrum of the crowd mixed with hotdogs, nachos, and three ice-cold Cokes knocked me out. It was a valiant fight between my eyeballs and eyelids during the seventh inning. A hot palm brushed across my forehead woke me as the crowds streamed up the stairs to reveal rows and rows of vacated seats filled with dirty nacho containers and crushed drink cups fluttering in the hot night breeze.

The next morning at a diner, just the sight of a steaming, buttery short stack made me queasy. I picked around the edges, never seeming to make a dent. My dad waited for me to surrender before he slid my plate in front of him and dug in. He drank his coffee in quick, powerful swallows between bites. We didn't talk much. I sat up tall in the booth and kept my feet still, except I wanted to be in the car and headed home. I was ready to go. I didn't miss my mom, trusting that she would be there and things would return to the way they had always been before the Dad-and-Rebecca baseball weekend. I was ready to go home.

As he poured more coffee for himself from the pot the waitress had set on the table, I can't explain it, but in that moment I saw myself for the first time. It was if the future me—more grown up—was looking from across the room and seeing my little girl uncombed hair and eyes thick with sleep. I was growing up and moving toward Dad's side of the table: eating mounds of food and drinking pots of coffee. Someday I would be the one who paid the bill, fit the keys in the ignition, and followed the road signs from Kansas City across endless miles.

It was sad to leave my little kid self behind in the booth. On the other hand, I was sure that I would know what needed to be done when I was in my dad's world.

He drank more coffee, and I ached for him, my big handsome goofball of a dad. I had called him *Daddy*, but from that moment in the diner on, he was Dad. I wanted to tell him that he didn't have to worry about me because I was a big girl who could take care of herself. I wanted to fast forward and be with him: funny and capable and grownup. Both of us drinking coffee and ready for a long drive home. Instead I started to bounce, tiny beats up down up down, on the booth's cold plastic seat.

Soon after, when my dad and mom split up, he moved out of the house and across town. My mom hadn't wanted to witness him pack up his stuff and she didn't want me to see it either. I wasn't there to see my dad pick the pants he would need. I didn't see him select a sensible number of socks and underwear.

Instead I saw him pack his suitcase the morning after the Royal's game that summer before fifth grade. My things were mostly still neatly folded in my bag. (I wore jeans, rolled at the cuff and a Royals T-shirt.) My dad's bag had exploded on the bureau next to the television. Socks and T-shirts cascaded down the half-open drawers. While I zipped my suitcase, he grabbed things and shoved them inside his bag. I didn't let him carry my suitcase. Mom had taught me that a girl should pack what she can carry with her own two hands. I said, *It's okay, Daddy, I can carry it fine.* He said my mother had always been a sensible girl too.

When I imagine Dad packing his bags to leave our house less than a year later, I worry that he took what he found scattered. He took the mess from his closet floor and shoved it into a few bags and lugged them himself to his car. I often wonder if he stopped in a diner to eat pancakes that first morning when he woke up after he left us. But I wasn't there to watch him pour his coffee or lick just the tips of his syrupy fingers, while he winked at his little girl. He took his clothes with him, but left all the photo albums at the house. (Maybe he expected to come back, I used to think.)

I still have the tiny wooden bat I got for free that night at the game. I keep it on a shelf next to a picture of my fourth-grade self—a girl with an intent smile, her lips drawn against her teeth for minimal exposure. There is no picture of Dad on my shelf, so why should he have a picture of me on display in his apartment? It is silly to waste my time trying to imagine his apartment. He moves often and never takes me to his newest place. He tells me that he is terrible at cleaning up; it's better for us to hang out somewhere else where we can get French fries.

That's Dad. His genes (and mine) are programmed to eat hot, salty fries.

We eat the fries in silence. Both of us lost in our own thoughts. I don't tell my dad much about guys. He doesn't ask. I talk about school, homework, and music. (We both like classic rock.) He always asks about Tiffany and Luke. I talk about topics that are light and bright and make the time we share easy to bear. When I see him check his watch, I yawn and say I have lots of homework today. He gives me his best "work hard in school" Dad face. I smile my best "you can count on me to be on the honor roll" smile and shrug my shoulders.

When he drops me off, I give his hand a little squeeze and slide out the car door.

HEAD GAMES

Truth: About me, about how I fool around. Have hooked up. I can't put it into textbook words, even though I know all of them. It makes me sad, a little bit. With Luke it was always just Luke. With other boys, it was something else. It was about their friends, it was about proving something, it was about making sure the after-talk made you into something worth the hype: a balance between knowing how (crucial) and knowing who to blow and how often. Head games.

I am finished with hooking up and finished with research. A girl can only take so much research. There is a moment in the mental note-card making when one's mind goes: Stop. Drop. Write the college essay.

Or in my case: Stop, drop, and do something. Luke told me. He told his best friend. What if this had happened to me? What would I want Luke to do for me? If I told him, I would want him to fix it. Make it go away. Make Weston pay. And not necessarily in that order.

I do not know how to make Weston pay.

I need a plan. I need to make a list.

YOU DON'T HAVE TO TELL ME

It is the night before I leave for Florida on Christmas break. Luke is at my house, helping me pack. He rolls my socks in tight cylinders and tucks them into my shoes. He isn't talking much, at first. Then,

–I want to, Rebecca.

–If you want, okay.

–There is more. I didn't tell you everything about that night. Are you mad at me?

–What on earth for?

–For not telling you the whole thing. What if this changes? It is awful. I am so sick, such a loser.

–Luke, look me in the eyes.

We stay like that until his breathing calms. I wonder if he remembers when he looked me in the eyes and saw into me for the first time.

The thing is: Luke doesn't remember us from back in the eighth grade. He is letting me slip away from him. He isn't trying to keep me in his head. It's like the more trash he tells me, the lighter his load. He drives away from each conversation having shed another skin. He gets thinner and brighter in the bargain.

Luke again tells me his story, in his own words. This time the story has changed.

Everything happened like I said, Luke begins. Except, I had vodka too. When we got there, before the beer. They had this funnel and Roger put it in Weston's mouth, and then Weston held it there while Roger poured vodka from the bottle. Then it was Roger's turn. Then it was mine. Roger gave me the funnel. I put it between my teeth, and vodka slid down my throat. I tipped my head back further, and then Weston pulled me into a chair. I thought he wanted Roger to pour the vodka into the funnel faster. Weston pushed my shoulders down, grabbed my arms, and held both my wrists in a real tight grip twisted behind me so I couldn't move. Then Roger started to pour. It burned like fuck. It was so quiet there. No electricity at the cabin; no music. The stars were so bright that night—we went out to piss—and I remember thinking the stars were a galactic band—with percussion, the horns, backup singers, three keyboards and dancers. Who needed music when I had my own private lead singer—the waxing moon lit up by prairie fires. The whole sky jamming out inside my head.

When Weston held me down like that with my wrists in his fists, it was like being touched by—Jennifer Lopez or Catherine Zeta-Jones, or Michael Jordan or the president of the United States. You know, Weston chose *me* to hang out at the lake. All the kids would know. It would be smooth. Becca, it felt good. I was ecstatic just to be there, near him. When he started calling me a fag, it was all crazy, you know? When he asked me if I had a girlfriend, he took out his dick and started saying how it was "candy" and how girls would pay to suck him off. He said, "That's the way it is supposed to go: girls taking what they get." Then he said, "I know about Justin." And I didn't know what he meant. "What are you talking about?" I said. He said he knew that Justin was a "cocksucker." Then he hit me the first time. Then he hit me again. He told me to take off my jeans. Then he started to jerk off. I had my pants half down; I was off my head drunk. And, Becca, I am so sorry, so sick, but—my dick was hard. He smiled. I tried to smile; I tried to cover it up; I tried to play it off. That knife. "Faggot," he said. "Sicko, you deserve what you get." He had me down, his hands tight around my arms. He tore me up real bad. I closed my eyes. I pretended it was a nightmare. I said to myself: No, this is not happening, this is not happening. I didn't scream. I didn't want Roger to come back inside. The last thing I wanted was Roger to see us like that. Do you get that, Bec? Do you? If Roger had come back in there, I would be dead now. I would have killed myself. In the bathroom, after, the blood poured out my nose, and my dick was still hard. I locked the door. I locked myself in because I wanted to grab Principal Ames's hunting knife and carve it—my own dick—off.

–Luke,

–yeah

–Luke, it was not your fault. He raped you.

When I say *rape,* he shudders and presses his fingertips into his forehead. His thumbs plug his ears.

–The other stuff doesn't matter. What Weston did was wrong.

–yeah

–Luke, I'm real sorry. (And I am so, so scared.)

–yeah, me too.

REBECCA ALONE

I am furious. This is anger. This is being burned alive by silence. This is the world vomiting into my mouth. A bitter, rancid stream of its failure. After Luke leaves, I take my spiral notebooks—the careful accounting of my high school curriculum—down from the shelf. I tear the pages out, one page at a time. I make a fire on the backyard patio.

Burn Etruscans. Burn Judicial-Legislative-Executive. Burn Endocrine System. Burn Checks-and-Balances. Burn Sappy-Ass Poems. Burn Sex-Ed and DARE. I don't even unfold the creased page that has the poem I wrote for Luke. I can't bear to see it. It was written for a Luke who doesn't exist. It was written by a Rebecca I want to forget. It burns. The words are lost.

The fire burns and meanwhile my mom's little blue tablets keep her dead asleep. The fire leaves a black welt on the cement. The patio couch covers it neatly. I sit there and freeze, frozen on fire, breathing smoke. Breathing smoke from my words.

Luke was raped. That is bad enough. He can't tell anyone but me. If he tells the police or his parents, he might as well die. If he tells, he will be tainted for the rest of his life: People will think he is gay. No matter what the truth may be, the sideways glances, the whispers, the outright scorn for acts against human nature, will become part of his life. You can't escape what others think about you. Once judgment is passed, you are bound to serve a life sentence in its shadow. Memory is long and condemnation a favorite pastime despite the tidy lawns.

Weston attacked him—had "sex" with him—to him. Weston must think that Luke is gay. That's why he did it. Punishment for the weak. Weston remembers that kid, Justin, who must have been gay. Justin hit on Luke; followed him around. Weston noticed. Why did he attack Luke? Was it a game? A test? A perverse flirtation? A show of strength? Rough house gone criminal?

What people will think: Luke gave it up with a guy. Luke went to the cabin. He drank a few beers and a lot of vodka—through a funnel. He asked for it. What will people think of Weston? They won't believe that he did it. They won't believe Luke's story. They will see Weston as that tough guy, who maybe roughed him up.

What if Luke had to tell his story on the stand? Impossible. This I know.

For 76 days (weekdays and weekends) Luke's story has thumped in my head like some crazy house party with techno music and a beat that pounds into me without a break, without a redeeming lyric to uplift the spirit. No rising strings. No hard rock screams. Not a soothing ballad to be heard. Just pound, pound, pound.

You see it in movies all the time: girl gets beaten/raped/left for dead and gets crazy-mixed in the head and in the end finds her voice to tell. Boy rapist gets handcuffs. We walk out of the theater thrilled. The sex-violence coupled with the justice neat and tidy. But there is no movie script here. I have to write my own. I have to end this. I have to connect the dots, read the evidence, and whip-snap-surprise-ending make the audience feel safe in their seats. I have to make it right.

Why? Because: Luke did not deserve it. Luke, my darling, my sweet, my friend. Friends stick together; they come through when things are bad. I never knew the terrible price of that cliché, until now. Friends do more than write a sappy poem or give cheesy birthday presents.

This is I know: When Luke kisses me I am alive. I am home. He makes me feel soft and full. He makes me feel. Just feel. I can't explain it. Yet it is true, the way he kisses me. It means something. It feels alive. I feel alive when we kiss.

It was true. He will never kiss me that way again. I will never be kissed that way again.

What Weston did was not "sex." Whatever sex is, it is not what happened at the lake. It was a kind of murder. He might as well have used the hunting knife.

The words are burned. The fire is long gone. The air reeks of smoke. I go back in the house chilled to the bone. I strip down and get in a hot shower. The water scalds my skin. I wash my hair; let the conditioner set. Sitting on the shower floor, the water stings my neck as I hang my head between my knees.

I think about Weston. That night at the party with Tiff, sophomore year. When Lucy was there.

I am so thick:

Lucy. Why did Lucy—strong-minded, long-limbed—Lucy, leave town? Was she pregnant? Or was she worse than pregnant? Do other kids gag when they see Weston at the end of the hall? What if he does it again to Luke? What if he does it again to another boy? Another girl?

I have to make Weston pay for what he has done. However I accomplish it, no one can know the truth about what happened to Luke. I will bear the secret.

I promised, no repeats.

I was sure that Weston should pay for his sin. Now I am sure that Luke is not able to do it. I am sure of this, finally. I am sure that I, Rebecca Alone, will make Weston pay.

The water goes cold. I let it run cold. My skin ripples beneath its assault.

GRANDMA'S HOUSE

It's a relief to go to Grandma's house for Christmas break. Grandma moved to Florida when I was six years old. We used to come here for Christmas with Dad. Now it is just Mom and I on the long car trip. Mom and me and the tension that accumulates in a magnetic field around the radio dial. This year my mom let me drive most of the way. The best part of getting to drive: my mom sleeps like the dead and I can tune in to classic rock or tinny pop to my heart's content.

There are two levels in Grandma's condo. She sleeps upstairs facing the sea while my mom takes the spare bedroom facing the parking lot. I sleep on the pullout downstairs. When I wake up to the winter sun, I love to wrap my afghan around my chest and walk to the patio door to check on the sea. Each time I rise, the sea remains. I am not sure why this confounds me. It is always there. It remains. After the first two nights, I hardly notice the surf even though I know it remains, tossing foam and sea spray, while I dream.

Today I will go for a walk along the water, collect bits

of sea glass for my collection. My mom convinced me years ago that Grandma would love to keep my prized gems here in Florida. As if it were a favor to Grandma, who keeps them in a cylinder glass tube in the spare room. I move the jar to the patio, where I can add to it after a walk. The sun glints green and blue first thing in the morning. There is a layer of shells in the jar—a summer fling with the mollusk back in ninth grade. I love that jar.

Mom is sacked out still at 9 a.m., like usual when we are in Florida. She goes days without a shower. Pajamas by day. Late night TV. Naps in a lounge chair with a trashy novel blocking the sun. Mom and I laze about while Grandma makes oatmeal for breakfast. Later, there will be iceberg salad for lunch. For dinner, she has a list of meals we rely on: meatloaf, salmon casserole, mushroom chicken, and always steamed broccoli.

This year I don't get sucked into the surf-induced laze mode. Grandma stands behind my chair and tut-tuts to see me reading and highlighting, scrawling quotes and numbers on 5 x 7 lined note cards. She had never seen me work at anything. In Florida, the rule: sun. Back in Kansas, we have a different rule: wind. The incessant winds lash at your skin, defeating all except the most resilient hair sprays. When in Florida, mom and I sink into the white noise of the pounding surf. We can hear it in our chests, but it stays mercifully away from the skin.

The college essay can no longer be avoided. A persistent fact: application deadlines are January 15th. I have a manila folder for each college's admission requirements. I have extra copies of my transcript sealed up and official. I have the solid choices lined up and the back-up options. I asked Ms. Walters to send letters of recommendation. My sure-bet colleges: KU. University of Kansas—Go Jayhawks, et cetera. I am sure that KU will accept me, and I might score a scholarship. My mom went there. My dad went to K State. I should apply to K State, even though my dad didn't push it. He says I should apply where I think it would good for me—where I can have fun too. Mom rolled her eyes when I told her Dad said that.

KU has a better college town, as far as I can tell. I was on campus for a yearbook/journalism conference sophomore year. Then my mom took me for a visit at the end of junior year. When she left me there for Friday and Saturday night, I saw the dorms, went to a class, and talked to students. I spent both nights with a girl—Jennifer Miller—who had signed up to host *prospectives*, as she called us. She was very busy and used a planner to account for each hour of the day for weeks in advance. Homework. Reading. Parties. Treading the *mill* at the gym. She studied at the *'brare* and loved group projects. (Truth: I wanted to be her. Do her assigned reading, make salient points in class. Ask probing questions in an anthropology lecture. She had a stash of cranberry vodka under her bed. She had her own mini sink and vanity. She curled her eyelashes before class. She had flip-flops to wear in the hall shower. (She let me borrow them.) I wanted to skip my senior year, cram my belongings into a dank dorm room, and start college.)

Why the endless application paperwork? Why the tiny, tiny boxes with similar options?

If I get the application in on time, I'll have a fighting chance to own my very own shower flip-flops, carry a shower tote. I need to focus on that, worry about scholarships later.

First the acceptance, then the details, I tell myself. *We'll work out the details, Rebecca*, my mom's refrain. Get the big stuff done and then I can afford to obsess about the endless details. I smile at her. What else can I do? She is glad to see me buckle down during vacation. *That's the price I have to pay for pretending the applications would write themselves,* she says.

Next: Kansas Newman—Go Jets. A small Catholic school. I promised Tiff that I would apply there, her top choice. Her dad went there. Third: Harvard. Go Crimson. Why not? There is a teeny-tiny chance I would get accepted, but no way can we afford it. And if I never apply, I'll never know. Worst-case scenario: I'll have to turn them down if Mom and Dad can't foot the bill. Aim high. Where is Cambridge anyway? I thought Harvard was in Boston. Grandma convinced me to apply to FSU. Go Seminoles. I like the idea of being here for college, near Grandma's green salads and salmon casserole. Except, I can't imagine studying in so much sun.

Finally, all the blanks are filled. All the boxes are checked. I settle into writing my essay. I have a detailed outline and notes from during the semester. Ms. Walters's voice reverberated in my head.

I pack my bag and drive to the local library.

I pass an extensive paperback selection near the door. Sand grit falls from between the pages as I glance through a few titles. There is the usual cast of public library crazies, whose eye contact I avoid, as I make my way toward the public computers. I sit. I log in. I take out my notes. I clean my fingernails. I make little notes on my outline. I look at the ceiling. I check my email: nothing from Luke. No surprise. Still. So, I write the Essay.

The Essay: solid work. A bit of flare even. Textbook punctuation with a semicolon here and there just to show I can. I didn't give up on Mother Jones. I hope invoking her name does the trick. I'll ask Grandma to edit my first draft.

As it prints, I take a walk on the wild side and mentally check off the essay. It is nearly done anyway. Day after tomorrow I'll mail the batch. Then wait. When school starts I will engage in long, drawn-out agonizations in homeroom about what-ifs, I hopes, and whatever. There will be the shame of rejection, and the smugness of multiple acceptances. Now: I wait. In the meantime, Grandma will make me cheesecake with fudge and cherries to celebrate my eleventh-hour diligence.

Colleges make decisions based on transcripts and the letters of rec written before Christmas break. I bank on that.

READING DANIELLE STEEL

It was a normal Christmas celebration for us girls down in the Florida sun. We baked Christmas sugar cookies and spent hours lost in the frenzied mall crowds. I got Mom a new fuzzy robe and a glass flower vase for Grandma. Dad sent me Zeppelin's greatest hits. Mom gave me a couple of Danielle Steel novels.

I need to read about a soap opera instead of star in one. I need bad things to happen to good people followed by a happy ending.

On the patio, my pale arms and alabaster cheeks under the white sun, I tuck a blanket around my legs and sip hot mint tea. Grandma dries mint from the farmer's market for her famous tea, which she swears by and mails to all her sisters. Mom gulps coffee (cream and sugar, two teaspoons) by the 16-ounce refillable thermal mug. The coffee/tea divide. Mom drinks less coffee here. I drink more tea.

Mother Jones Essay: done.

Applications: check.

Christmas: celebrated. Well, not quite. I still have to

honor Santa with Tiff and Luke, but I haven't picked out their gifts yet. It is easy to get stuff for the family. It takes longer to hone in on just the right thing for my friends. Mom loves anything I get for her and will use it religiously, even the hideous burnt orange lipstick I bought her when I was 16 and ashamed of her palest pink when everyone else was into earth tones. I think I will treat Tiff to a manicure, even join her and get dolled up with long, girly, hot pink acrylics. A girl can use a new set of daggers. Tiff will love it: just the two of us at the mall. I'll take her before letters descend from the four corners of the collegiate world, before we start the buildup to prom. There will be boutonnieres to consider. (Not to mention the boys we need to pin them on.)

Luke needs so much. Yet seems to want so little. What can I get him for Christmas? I already volunteered to write his college essay. I offered to fill out his applications. I told him that Mom was a bona fide expert on financial aid forms. I knew my Mom would help Luke if he would let me ask. Luke told me, *No way. I got it. No thanks.*

Luke refused all of my attempts to quote unquote fix his future. That is what he calls it. That is how he sees it. He said he needed to concentrate on the test this Friday (or this coming Monday, or that makeup assignment); next week, next semester, next year would have to wait until he got there.

Luke wasn't the only kid to miss the first round of deadlines. This is why colleges have rolling admissions: for kids who roll over in bed one Saturday noon and realize that Mommy will not change their sheets forever. I want Luke to go to college. I need him to go. I always thought that we would go to KU, even Tiff. The three of us. Now more than ever I want them to be with me, in a new place, with a new start. Which is silly. I slosh a bit of tea onto the white embroidered edge of the blanket as I shift in the lounge chair. There is no reason to be alarmed at the minor spill, and I trace a daisy on the familiar throw Grandma bought for my visits. The tea saturates a single daisy. No worries. A bit of spilled tea is not a tragedy. Hardly.

I will gift Luke with my slave services for his graduation party. It is the one thing he talks about anymore. Of course, that can't be my real Christmas present because I already promised him as much. It is supposed to be "our" party. We got Melissa to go in with us. Tiff is out. I want out too. But I won't back out on Luke. Tiff will be there and enjoy the party and be in all our pictures. But. She is not officially a co-host because her family will have a "small gathering on the lawn" with a tent and catered food the next day. They had similar gatherings for her older brothers and sister. She is the last of the tribe to walk the graduation line in the shiny black gown with her mortarboard askew. Her parents expect her to wear the gold cords of the honor society around her neck. She will. (So will I, hopefully.)

Her parents felt that it was unfair to Luke and me (and Melissa) to overcommit. We are invited to her party too, of course. Her parents will make an appearance at our party, a ten-minute breeze-by with discreet envelopes for the gift table.

When Tiff told Luke and me about her parents' decision, she apologized. This was a first. She was genuinely embarrassed by what her parents had done. I could see it in her face. She said she wanted to scream about the stupid tent that they had rented without telling her. It was December when they put down a deposit to secure the reservation. She settled for a week or two of one-word replies to their pointed questions about her day at school before she got tired of her show of force.

We love Tiffany. She is the spoiled baby of her family and of our little friendship-family too. We hate to see her squirm. We love to see her glow. I am sorry she felt torn between her parents and us. About a party. It seems so ridiculous, sad. Luke and I told her not to worry about it.

I turn my thoughts from Tiffany's glow to my novel. The cover has an impossibly romantic couple embracing next to an airplane. The Danielle Steel novel is thick, the font not too smallish.

The beautiful girl in the novel is unaware of her stunning good looks. She is headstrong and talented beyond all comparison. She wants to fly airplanes despite her father's conviction that girls don't fly, it ain't seemly. The man is scandalously older, yet he is born to fly, just like her. He teaches her against her father's wishes. It is clear that the feisty girl and the wizened older man are cut from the same cloth, birds of a feather, peas in a cockpit. Good people to whom bad things are destined to happen, and whose love will prevail and resolve on the last page. Sip tea. Turn page. Nap until the breeze stirs the hairs at the nape of my neck.

Sip. Turn. Love takes flight in between the pages of a romance novel. Characters destined to love despite the odds, despite the costs, love.

Sip tepid tea. Nap, and dream:

I am a tour guide at a museum version of my high school. I am frantic to explain that the gold-embossed plaque of Luke Warren with the dates 1985–2002 means that Luke was a student at Plains High until 2002, the year he graduated. A lady in sensible shoes and a red cardigan cackles. Everyone knows that if you have two dates separated by a dash it means that the person was born in such-and-such year and died in that year. I slap her face. The police arrest her for lewd behavior. She is hauled away, cackling. The tour moved down the hall. But I shout after them to come back, that I am *right* and she was crazy. They don't turn around. They pretend they can't hear me. Or they can't hear me. Then I see: a fleet of soft-soled sensible leather shoes. Women in red cardigans and comfortable shoes fill the halls. They don't look at me. But they agree: Luke is dead. And they don't care. I slip into the crowd. If he is dead, I am free.

Cold to the bone, I wake.

I let my heart rate calm and then open my Danielle Steel novel. "I love you Taylor. You taught me how to love, simply and true, before the world showed me that love isn't always enough to hold two people together." I apply the salve of literary romance to soothe the throb behind my eyes.

Grandma brings out the teapot dressed in its crochet tea cozy and refills my mug. We watch seagulls skitter about the sand with shells in their beaks. She narrates her neighbor's unfortunate predilection for beef dishes that require large amounts of garlic and sautéed onion. A lovely lady, really. Real nice. But the cooking fumes are repellent. Thank the Lord for ocean breezes.

THE LAST SUPPER

We leave for Kansas tomorrow before 8 a.m. It will be flapjacks and burgers all the way home. Tonight mom wants something from the sea. Grandma doesn't do flounder. So we load up in the car. It is a family-owned place, near the shore. A neighbor told Grandma about it ages ago, but she hadn't felt like going alone.

Mom orders the oysters. Grandma sticks to salmon. I go for the shrimp.

In honor of our last supper, Mom got rid of her house clothes and slipped into fresh jeans with a white-pilled sweater, for the chill. She wears the tiny shell-shaped earrings Grandma gave her for Christmas. Her right leg is crossed, and her foot bobs, showing off her dressy beach sandals (which will go into hibernation once we hit the plains). Grandma has on slacks and a no-iron cotton/polyester blend top in a soft peach floral. My mom is a younger version of Grandma, but harder in the face and joints. There is something resolute about her elbows that defy description. My mom's face—the grim mouth and glint in her tired eyes—never lets you forget that she is bearing up as a single mom. (Yet, she divorced my father. It was her idea. She kicked him out.) She wears motherhood like a pair of tight shoes. She loves me fiercely. Yet a part of her is locked up, waiting. For what, I'm not sure. I used to think that once she had me settled in my college dorm, she would go places. Go on dates in candlelit restaurants. Now I see her sitting here with Grandma, and I see the two of them: two old ladies, waiting for the sun to set. They might as well wait in Florida and enjoy the view.

The salads arrive: iceberg with hearts of palm doused with vinaigrette. Mom asks Grandma if she wants to fly up for my graduation. Mom and I know that Grandma is happy for me, but. It is a long trip, and her knees clench up in midair, taking days and weeks to soften into compliance. And besides, the airlines now are so ridiculous. There are long lines with screenings, and security checks, and you can't even bring your nail file on board without getting a pat down by some nasty man who landed his badge and walkie-talkie because of the desperate rush to hire bodies to fill the security ranks.

Our waitress takes our empty plates. She balances the dirty plates on her tray and hefts the whole mess toward the kitchen. She manages to look graceful. She is my age, I guess. A sheet of light brown hair in a perfect ponytail disappears behind a wooden door. At her ears she wears two tiny silver half-moons. I rub my own earlobe and imagine I have the courage to ask her where she bought her earrings.

–Dear, next year, what will you major in?

I am glad Grandma asks me about next year. It is good to hear myself lay out high expectations. How the first-year schedule is predetermined by requirements: literature, a math class, and maybe sociology, Spanish. I want to take Intro to Law or maybe a government class, because lately I have been considering law school. Mom raises her eyebrows; it is news to her (and me).

This law school version of me sounds impressive. Grandma is impressed with her salmon, which has a delicate dill sauce and fresh green beans on the side.

Mom and Grandma chat about Grandma's brother and sister; vague faces and names catch my attention. They live back in Missouri, where Grandma is from. I don't see them much. They send cards. Mom reminds me to include them when I order my graduation announcements. I stab a shrimp.

The shrimp are not the breaded, deep fat-fried popcorn variety. In fact, they have feet. (Who knew?) Each one has lots of spidery claws. I pick at them, wipe my fingers after every amputation.

Law school is not an entirely new idea. I thought about being a lawyer long before this trip, as far back as elementary school. I raised my hand when the teacher asked who wanted to be a lawyer because this other kid—Stephen—raised his hand. I always finished my math sheets first; Stephen was always moments behind me. My hand shot up when I saw him start to gesture. The rest of the year, Ms. Morgan always called me the class lawyer. If Ms. Morgan thought I am smart enough to be a lawyer, then why not? On the other hand, the frogs in biology class were just an aphrodisiac of what the sciences could offer me: next, pigs (cats, I heard) and then medical school and a human cadaver. Then, I, Doctor Rebecca, healer of the sick and lame. I don't tell my mom and Grandma about this alternative biological trajectory. We are eating, after all.

–I heard from Luke's mom, by the way.

I set my half-legged shrimp carcass on my plate. My head splits open. I wipe my palms on my napkin, dab my mouth, and engage the doe eyes—wide with wonder and blinded by the sun. Why did Luke's mom call? What does she know?

I want to ask what Luke's mom had to say.

I want to tell her what I know.

I want Luke to have told his mom and now here it is: my opening, my release.

I don't have to be a Judas after all. I don't have to betray Luke with a kiss.

Even if Luke's mom said nothing, I want to tell. Here in Florida where the sun will shine. Where old, soft bodies in flame-retardant pantsuits have seen it all. They are beyond the taint. This is my opportunity to let my Grandma cover my hand with her papery fingers and tell me that I am the best friend Luke could ever have. She'll say, That poor, poor boy. Mom will be distraught and embarrassed, but she will believe me. I am a good kid. She will tell me how to make it right. At least, she will listen.

–I told her Mexican food was just fine for the party?

–Fine.

–Fine? Good then, that's settled. I'll pay for the party plates, drinks, and such,

She rummages in her purse for something. She finds a tissue and blows her nose.

–Grandma, you should come. It would be nice to have you at graduation.

In fact, it would be better if she stayed here in the sun,

where she is happy. I don't tell her that she wouldn't be missed at the party. My mom would never forgive me. And my mom works hard, she needs her vacation; she needs her downtime here in Florida. She is a single mom, after all. The seafood stink changes into something I can feel on my skin, a surge at the back of my throat.

–My stomach, I need to be sick.

I run to the bathroom where I puke up tiny, perfect little fish legs.

We skip the fresh key lime pie.

In the car the next morning, when I am still queasy, my mom launches into a mother-daughter discussion about being "intimate" with boys. I wonder if she is terrified I have morning sickness. Whatevs. If only I were nauseated from pregnancy instead of malignancy.

I have been sick lately, that's true. I tell her, *I am fine, fine, fine.*

Not to worry. I am fine. I am fine with a capital F.

I am fine. I am headed back to Kansas. I am a girl who deep-down wants to do the right thing. I want to drink coffee, black. I want to drive a green jeep. I want to go to college. I want truth to be bright and shiny. I want to forget. But the truth is not beautiful. I cannot forget.

So I drive. I drive five miles per hour over the speed limit. I wear sunglasses. I swallow the bitterness. I smile at the right time. If I were a poet, I would know what not to say. I say nothing about what matters. The truth cannot find its way into words. I hate being a fake. But I am good at it. Doomed to succeed.

CHAPTER FOUR

FIRST BASE

Tiffany comes by the night before we return to school. I have lost seven pounds since school started in September. When I think of Weston, I puke.

Tiff notices my slim waist and the sad sag in my jeans. There are little gasps of jealous oohing and tsk-tsking at the sight of a gap between my waistband and my hipbone. She declares she must diet like a champion for prom (which she always says with a capital P and an excited gleam in her eye). I tell her that it was simple: I've been eating less, drinking milk, and no French fries. She believes me. She raises an arched brow and shakes her finger at me, telling me that I may be getting too skinny if that is possible.

She believes that I am not eating fries. There is history here. She trusts my will power—a force of Rebecca nature she has seen me exert in the past.

Last summer: I mastered self-control—at least Tiffany sees it that way. She was there to witness the event of the summer season. My softball team always wins, we have since sixth grade. Other teams scorned our black and silver

Hawks emblem. We had the best coach, the best hitters, and the best pitcher in the state. No joke. In fact, we had grown bored with winning. That is why we traveled, to find solid competition.

I started out as pitcher, back in the early days when we switched from coach-pitch into regular ball. After a season that saw too many walks and not enough strikeouts, I was switched to first base. It's the long legs. Anything thrown my way is within my reach. Sometimes I do the splits, keep my left foot tagged to the base and stretch my glove to snag a wild throw. Our shortstop is accurate but hotheaded and a show-off. When she has a fight with her boyfriend, watch out. Michelle zings bullets, except not at me, unfortunately. I have to use my full height and pivot on my center of gravity to catch what she dishes up.

Last summer, we lost. And lost again. Instead of a team, we divided into two factions. I sustained faction-free status for the first two weeks of the silent-treatment brawl. Then my shortstop slapped me across the face.

–You bitch.

Thwack. Her hand made a comical sound as it struck me. I didn't hit back. I was stunned. In fact, I was embarrassed for her, mostly. I felt my cheeks heat with shame at the whole scene. People watched from the stands. Parents and friends and guys we knew. Tiffany thinks I did nothing, said nothing, because I controlled myself, acted all mature, and didn't sink to Michelle's level. The truth: time froze, and I took the easy way out, which was to do nothing, say nothing. I just touched my face where her open palm had struck. Michelle immediately apologized. I said, Okay. It's okay. Forget it. You were mad. It's okay.

She smacked me because I didn't catch her latest wild bullet.

She slapped my face because her boyfriend broke up with her.

She humiliated me because he broke up with her when he found out that she had told another girl on the team that I flirted with him (which was a lie). I don't know why she lied about it. She probably wanted to dump him. She was talking up ways to make it happen. Planting rumors in her own head. She wanted to turn him into some kind of two-timer. I was a convenient scapegoat. People would believe that I flirted with him.

Michelle didn't mean to hurt me. She just wanted out of the game, with him, I mean. She wanted to break up but didn't know how to do it. I had dropped her wild throw, missed the third out. The next batter hit a home run. We had a few more innings to pull out the win. We didn't. We lost. And things changed after that. We used to care about the game, but after that we started to care more about not losing. And we continued to lose.

Sophomore year: Once my mom came to school and complained to Principal Ames about the rancid gym teacher, who had been generous with the B's. He claimed that we were all lazy jerk-offs and told us not to be surprised when report cards came out. We shrugged it off as an idle threat. But then the report card came home. B in gym. I nearly died with mortification. My mom fumed with righteous anger at the gym teacher. Then she scheduled a private meeting with Principal Ames. I was out of the room when she made that call. She didn't say a word about it to me.

When Principal Ames called me into the office, my

mom had been there to make her case and was long gone. He shook my hand. He sat me down. He proceeded to check things off a list with a controlled flick of his wrist while he told me he had met with my mother, "a lovely lady," and that my grade would be "fixed" to reflect my achievements during the weight-lifting unit. A silence sang. I fumbled to make sense of what he had said, of what my mother had done. Finally, I said, *Oh, thanks*.

Fact: I didn't deserve a B, and the coach was a loser. But to think that my mother had come here, behind my back, and pled my case. Incomprehensible. I was furious with the indignity of the situation. My mommy to the rescue. I wanted to kill my mother. Tiff and Luke listened, agreed with my fury, but Tiff said I should talk to her about it. Luke agreed. Instead I vented over multiple pie sessions at the diner about how she didn't even ask me, just butted in. Tiff said to talk to her instead of bitching about it. I wanted to screech at her, but screeching is her thing. I do not want to be a shrew. I do not want to sink to her level. Suck it up—that's my motto.

To this day Tiffany still thinks that I was cool-headed about it, not yelling at my mom about the grade issue.

So by now Tiffany believes in my ability to handle things: playing tournament ball and getting slapped in the face, my mother's good intentions gone ubermom, and, now, my ability to give up French fries for the sake of prom.

Prom v French Fries. No contest.

My "diet" is no diet. It is wretchedness, pure and simple, incarnate.

LINE DRIVE

New Year. New Semester. The first day of school. The first day of the rest of my life.

Some kids started a countdown to graduation on the physics chalkboard. When I arrive in class I can't keep my eyes off that descending number—90, 88, 86. I watch the countdown and my head expands with the idea that time is running out for us, for me, for Luke.

I have been preparing for graduation all my life. The yearbook will have a long list of accomplishments next to my senior portrait (which I still have to take by the February 22nd deadline, note to self):

> Student Council (1-4),
> Principal's Honor Roll (1-4),
> Student-to-Student Tutor Program (1-2),
> Perfect Attendance (1-3),
> Journalism/Yearbook (1-4), and
> Honor Society

It is too bad about the perfect attendance. Yet I have worked harder than most, and stuck with journalism/yearbook despite the long hours.

Tiffany and I signed up for Ms. Carver's journalism/yearbook class freshman year. Tiff dropped after a year. I kept it up sophomore year, and then what was the point of taking ceramics for only two years? I continued to crank out articles for the school paper as assigned. Not much news here. Sports scores, reunion announcements, scholarships, et cetera.

Junior year I volunteered to take pictures. The kid who had done it moved out of town. I stepped up. The photographer has to attend ten sporting events per semester. Snap some action photos, develop the film, and later pick the shots that make it into the yearbook. The goal: a diversity of action shots—catch 'em at the finish line, or with a tongue hanging out on the free throw line. Cheerleaders are different. I shoot them with perfect smiles and pom poms clutched at their hourglass waists.

I shoot. I take names, dates, and other pertinent details. All these facts will show up in cryptic captions beneath the images in the paper or yearbook.

Point. Shoot. At least, I like to take pictures. It's an excuse to go to the big Friday night game, alone. I wander the sidelines, see the athletes up close and sweaty. See calves flare, biceps pop, asses flex. I see the jock straps beneath the home team whites and feel, oddly, flushed at the sight.

I ride the bus to away games. I sit near the front, near the coach. I hear the athletes come to the coach's berth and make confessions, get absolved. A chuck on the shoulder blossoms into coach-talk eloquence. Beneath the private conversations between coach and athlete, there is a constant thrum of talk and laughter that intensifies in volume and hilarity toward a breathless summit. It peaks, and then, inevitably, there is a pregnant silence about 20 minutes before the bus rolls into the parking lot. The air tightens with pre-game nerves, thickens with aggressive hormones.

New Semester. Ms. Carver, our journalism/yearbook teacher, isn't here the first day. We shrug off the presence of the substitute. I research the pressing parking issue at Plains High. The next day there is yet another substitute. Then the news: Ms. Carver will not return.

It turns out that Ms. Carver has a mother in Vermont diagnosed with liver cancer. Ms. Carver is moving there to take care of her. It doesn't sound like her mother is going to get better. Bryan asks Ms. Carver if she will be back for prom. (She is the faculty co-sponsor.) She explains to him that she hopes she won't have a reason to come back this semester. *But Ms. Carver*, Bryan whines. He stops when I kick his chair.

I don't want her to go. I don't have a choice, however. I'm pissed. Do I have the right to be mad? I put in three-and-a-half years. Now she takes off and leaves me to wade through the end of senior year with some substitute.

I see her in the hall near the teacher's lounge after school. She holds a cardboard box of papers and office supplies.

–Ms. Carver, I just wanted to say, I'll miss you.

–I'll miss you too. The kids will count on you, Rebecca. You know the ropes. Help the substitute.

–Ms. Carver, I'm not sure I can. I mean, basketball is going to State, and we haven't sold enough ads yet, and half the football shots got overexposed. I am not good at selling ads, and who will copyedit the captions?

She doesn't put the box down.

I am not crying. I am not.

–Becca, do what you have to do. Give yourself a break, okay? At any rate, I have complete faith in you, honey. You work hard and you have a big heart. Okay?

The long-term sub shows up Monday morning. He is young (and a bit doughboy-ish, wears an ironed white button-down, khakis and a belt that would encircle at least six freshmen if he needed to corral the wild stallions in class). He sits down with me the first day, talks about who does what, deadlines, et cetera. I fill him in. He takes notes on a legal pad and says, "Sounds good!" at least once a minute. I watch him lift the table with his lumberjack legs when he shifts his weight.

As his pen fills yet another sheet of legal pad, an idea takes shape in my head. Journalism can be more than stories about the parking lot. I can report on the real news around here. I can propose a new series for the school paper. He is jotting down my every word, so I begin to reveal the paper's new series: Personal Personnel Profiles. I tell him I plan to start with the head office. I will spend class time immersing myself in the front office's day-to-day activities. It is about time students better understand the valuable work the secretaries and Principal Ames do for us. At such low pay.

He is sold at "low pay." It sounds like a solid project to him.

He assumes Ms. Carver already okayed this before she left for her family medical emergency.

I am golden.

IN THE KITCHEN

Luke's mom calls after school. She invites me for dinner on Saturday. She wants to test out a recipe for the graduation party. I have eaten her enchiladas and rice a good hundred times at least. She claims to have tried something new with the spices. She worries about guests who may not like spicy-hot Mexican foods. I tell her everyone loves her cooking, and the graduation party isn't for months.

The table is the only thing that stays in one place in Luke's dining room. Kids of all heights and stages of cleanliness bounce in their seats. Little Andrea has the biggest eyes and the smallest heart-pucker mouth. As I watch her grow older over the years, her eyes seem to register more and more astonishment, while her mouth stays a dandelion-blowing pucker. She is a charmer, my favorite.

She watches me all the time. I play footsy with her from across the table and she giggles, a little girl chime that makes everyone melt. We have played this game since before she can remember. I pretend to entertain her (but

I am the one entranced).

Luke tells us to knock it off. He knows I am the culprit. Andrea and I exchange a sly grin. She giggles more. Luke gets annoyed because as cute as Andrea is right now, ten minutes ago she was pulling toilet paper across the entire house. Ten minutes from now she will mount an anti-hand washing rebellion complete with an eardrum-shattering wail from her perfect pucker turned megaphone. Siren says, family does. She will wipe her greasy fingers down the hall in an escape maneuver. My favorite, precisely because I don't have to live with her, I'm sure. Luke will clean the grease with a soapy rag from the kitchen sink. His mom, already elbow-deep in suds, won't even have to ask him to do it as she turns her attention to her immediate conquest: pots and pans.

At least it was like that on previous nights at the Warren house. Tonight precocious Andrea eats her enchilada, her rice, and wipes her plate with a tortilla. I tell Mrs. Warren, Way to go. Whatever spice you added, it works for Andrea. She says, Rebecca you are so funny. (I am not funny.) She tells me five times that I am too skinny, eat more. More, Rebecca, more. Even as she leaves the table, More, Rebecca, and heads toward the kitchen to defeat the plates and dishes, the stovetop a battle ground of baked-on-cheese cast iron dishes. She sighs, a short but undeniable resignation, and moments later she vacates the kitchen. The dishes will wait. She puts half the troops in front of a Disney movie. Gets the other half in the tub, including Andrea with her arm floaters. Luke and I sit at the table, eat, and talk about the graduation party. I scrape up my last bit of sauce and beans. I belch. He says, You're welcome.

We go into the kitchen and Luke loads the plates in the dishwasher. I run hot water into the pots to start a good soak.

–Did you send in your college stuff?

I tell him, Yes, in fact. I tell him not to worry about *my* applications.

He doesn't retort.

–So, I am doing a new series for the paper. I'll interview faculty, coaches. Do a personal story about them. You know, why they teach, favorite books, music, movies, et cetera.

Luke stacks plates in the bottom rack.

–I am starting at the top, you know. Hanging out in the head office. To observe what really happens there. I want to get up close to Principal Ames.

The last plate in place, Luke picks up the dirty forks. He turns to me, bits of rice fly.

–What are you up to? What are you trying to do?

He hisses at me. I back up against the counter, turn toward the sink. I run the water full blast, let soap leak into the sink, watch the suds boil.

–I wanted you to know: I'm going to interview Ames. After all, he's our principal. Maybe the students could appreciate him if we know about the "real" man behind the desk.

I say this with false enthusiasm. Of course, I don't intend to make Ames into a good guy, obviously. I am not into public relations.

I just want to get near him.

Truth: I have no idea what to do. I don't know how to make Weston pay. I have to get closer to Ames. This is the best I can do. I keep my eyes open, look for a way, and hope that the pieces will fall into place. I can hope. And be ready. I feel like I am on the verge. I feel *this close* to something big. Ready to pounce.

–Rebecca, you sure you want to do this? I know it's for me.

–You've nothing to do with it.

That was a lie, I think.

THE CHAIR

I made the hair appointment two weeks ago knowing that we had a half-day at school. I planned to go home, get a round of homework done, and be at the salon with plenty of time to page through the magazines in the cramped, fragrant lobby. If I arrive before the normal afternoon rush, there is a much-improved chance to snag a fresh Vogue.

I want it short. No, I want a change.

I sit in the waiting area and use fluorescent stick-it notes to tab the luscious models whose precision bobs angle across their necks just so. Like punctuation. I like the sass of it. Never in my life had I thought I would go for the jaunty short do. But here I am.

Melinda, my hairstylist and my mom's since I was in a booster seat, tells me to come on back. She sees me haul thick fashion mags toward her chair. She asks me what I have in mind as she runs her fingers across my scalp, lifts my fine hair and gives it a good tousle. I tell her I was thinking of maybe doing something different. I am ready for change, I declare. It's good to say it, and bold. Bits of her last client's hair cling to the hair dryer she stashes away. Curls? Color? Color is the thing now, she agrees with me (even though I hadn't suggested it). She fastens my cape. I say, Short—a bob? She tells me, Oh honey. Let's think about this: First of all, your mother will kill me. Second, it is such a drastic change. Let me wash you. Then we'll talk.

Melinda has hair that impresses. It is deep chestnut and the curls bounce in long rivulets. She has bangs. She *still* has bangs, even though not a single model in any of the magazines have them anymore. My mom has bangs. Melinda, unlike my mother, carries the look well. Melinda reigns in the frenetic salon, with a royal air of delegation. Getting things done. Getting ladies done up. Getting girls out the door with updos. She favors black leggings and tunics. She crackles with good spirit. She and the other hairdressers talk about ordering in lunch, or where to all meet for dinner. Where to get drinks on Friday night (if it is Wednesday or Thursday) or where they had drinks (if it is Monday or Tuesday). I trust her with my hair.

I normally tell her things. I find the stories pouring out of me as she flits back and forth around me.

Today she says,

–Let's just trim you up, and, maybe, take off an inch? Trust me, honey. (Maybe that is why I trust her, she always tells me to).

–You will feel fresh and light. It will feel like a real change.

I feel like a coward, but I am relieved. My pits stop sweating and I sit up straight under the cocoon of the cape. I worry my hangnail.

Melinda asks me about school, about graduation,

about college, about Tiffany and Luke.

I tell her that I applied to KU and Kansas Newman. I don't mention Harvard, afraid she will think I am ridiculous. I go with the science major. "I plan to take biology and major in it, with a minor in law." She is impressed. So am I. She launches into a description about her high school biology lab experiments. It is hilarious the way she laughs at herself for getting out of doing any real work for the dissection unit. She coaxed her lab partner, a boy, into doing all the work. She didn't want to ruin her nails; now look at her! We laugh.

I feel blood ooze from my nail bed. I apply pressure and will myself to stop picking at it.

As I pay, Melinda reminds me to book real soon for prom. It will be a madhouse here, she says, and gives me a little hug. Her hands grip my shoulders and she blurts: Oh dear god, what if we had cut all your hair off before *prom*? Your mother would've just *killed* me.

Maybe we should invite Melinda to the graduation party. She would have a good time no matter what. She would eat enchiladas and make small talk with our parents. She would be a force of good energy. It would be fun to have her there. I still believe this party can be salvaged; it should be fun. We deserve that much.

HEAD OFFICE

On Monday I go to journalism and report to our doughboy wonder substitute, then head to the main office. I tell Mrs. Buckley about my journalism assignment. She has been a secretary here since before I arrived. She knows the ropes. She listens to my idea: I want to be a fly on the wall and then later interview a few staff members about their work and their lives outside of work. Hobbies, pets, et cetera. She listens with one ear, shuffles tardy slips in the other hand. Honey, she says, that sounds like a real good idea for the newspaper. She gives me a brief tour, pointing out which file cabinets are off-limits (and locked).

I settle down behind her desk with my notepad and camera. I sit on the floor so students who come in can't see me. Teachers and staff who pass through to check their mailboxes and make small talk won't see me unless they walk behind Mrs. Buckley's desk. They don't.

The secretaries work the phones. Parents call about sick kids, ask for homework assignments. Paper is pushed. There are deliveries—lots of them: flowers, cakes, even pizza for a fourth-hour history class. Unfair. The nurse stops by and leans her ample hip on Mrs. B's desk to chitchat about diarrhea. I kid you not. There is some kind of epidemic in the west-wing bathrooms. I remember back to elementary school when some kid or other was always puking up the hall or otherwise fouling the carpets. Principal Ames emerges from his office to meet a visitor. They shake hands and beam at one another.

Ames looks like he always does: navy pants, navy three-button blazer. His button-down shirt is white with thin blue stripes, pressed. Green tie. Brown loafers, shined up. He is the kind of dad who polishes his shoes. My dad was not. My grandpa used to polish his dress lace-ups on Sunday afternoons while I napped on the couch. The bristles loud against the leather, but just the right kind of loud to make me sleepy and dream about riding a train or a sailing on a boat under a summer sun.

I am tired. No, I am sleepy.

So I force myself to keep busy and jot down descriptions of each secretary, her outfit, and general characteristics. I draw a map of the room. The ancient wall clock actually, really, ticks each time the minute hand lurches forward.

The second hand spins. The minute hand lurches.

Ticklurch.

Ticklurch.

I take a few pictures of the office staff in action. One woman on the phone holds up a stack of papers. Another secretary clacks away on her ergonomic keyboard. Each woman puts on a smiling game face, but I can tell from the puzzled wrinkles between their brows that they are sure the pictures will be terrible or at least a waste of time. I disagree. They will radiate warmth and efficiency from the newsprint after I finish with the touching-up process.

Then I see the family photos. The smiley men and tiny babies (grandchildren?) slant next to modest potted plants and tiny American flags. These are fodder for questions, indeed. I will ask about the pictures in follow-up interviews. One secretary has her family—all three children frozen as toddlers or elementary school students—framed in primary colors.

My eyelids are heavy.

The right one weighs: one ton.

Ticklurch.

The left: two tons point five.

Mrs. Buckley looks at the clock, and declares: Who's ready for a fresh pot? She pushes her chair back to a round of cheers and goes to put the fresh coffee in the machine.

When she comes back with a steaming mug, I ask if I can join her. It is part of the immersion experience, I tell her.

I cradle the mug in my hands and let the steam open my pores. It is 2:45. School dismisses in 30 minutes. The staff stays until 4:30. I plan to stay until the staff leaves. Just to see what I can see.

Weston comes in at 4:23 to see his dad. Mrs. Buckley waves him in without calling first to see if Ames is busy. Weston doesn't see me sitting low behind Mrs. Buckley's desk. He stays until 4:27. He heads for the door, his black gym bag (ripe with the scent of old fruit and dead mice) bashes the corner of Mrs. Buckley's desk, inches from my face. He doesn't see me hidden there.

After the office door closes, I take up my Bic and write: nothing. I have nothing to write about what I have witnessed. He came to see his dad. He stayed for four minutes. I don't know what they said. His gym bag reeks. Not exactly noteworthy stuff.

Time to go. When I stand and unkink my legs, I go lightheaded with a rush of blood away from my brain. In a woozy haze I see Principal Ames leave his office, lock his door, and then rush toward me. He takes me by the elbow—a hot touch, but I can't tell if it is my heat or his— and guides me into a solid chair. Now the blood saturates my face. I am devastated by my untimely weakness.

He tells me to take it easy.

I say, I am fine, thanks.

We walk out the office door together. He uses his massive key ring to lock the double-wide glass doors behind us. We stand in the afternoon sun slant in the lobby. He tells me to "have a pleasant evening." He goes out the main entrance, striding through the bitter wind toward his car. I step behind a pillar and keep my eyes on him. He fastens his seat belt. He adjusts the heater or the radio. He drives away.

I have pages of notes. Including a map of the room detailing each secretary's desk. And a slight caffeine buzz. As I stuff the notes into my bag, I bite the inside of my cheek in one of those random muscle malfunctions. I implode with the pain. Stupid, stupid.

I OF THE STORM

Luke missed the first round of college-application deadlines.

He didn't take his senior portrait in time for the yearbook.

He is absent today, Monday, February 25th. Today we order caps and gowns. My homeroom teacher has been announcing this deadline for months, I swear. But this is the last, last deadline. He isn't at school.

He calls me the minute I get home. I ask him if he turned in the cap-and-gown form. He says he'll do it tomorrow. He tells me, Relax. There is always a way to get around those deadlines. He tells me he stayed home today to work on the party list: who gets invited and who doesn't. He cast a wide net, he tells me. There are freshmen from his swim club, who don't even go to our school. He has his dentist (who does go to his family's church). Melinda, my hairdresser, is included for my sake. I ask if he included my mom and dad on the list. He doesn't laugh. Wait, he says, and scans down the list and finds their names.

Luke reads the list. I half-listen as I pour a glass of milk, and kick my shoes under the table. Jessica Walters. Wait, Luke, repeat that. Who is that? He says, Ms. Walters, you know, Jessica Walters, our English teacher. I envision Ms. Walters as "Jessica" sipping punch in Luke's kitchen, making small talk with my mom. Then: Jill Turner. Who's that? He says, You know, she works at school.

–In the guidance office, Ms. Turner, she's kinda young, you know.

–She's in guidance?

–Yeah. A counselor, you know, college stuff, and stuff.

I sit down at the kitchen table. I put the phone to my other ear. I breathe. "And stuff." I know what this means, and my hands shake. I put my milk on the tabletop, jostling the glass enough to slosh milk over the lip. Spilt. Milk.

I don't ask him more questions.

He has said a lot.

It has been months (145 days) since he told me. I kept his secret, yes. But I have done nothing. I want to make Weston pay, make him bleed. But I am not that kind of girl. Not the type to scream at him in Main Hall, make a scene. Get suspension. I can't spread rumors to destroy him. He is a boy: he won't care about rumors anyway.

Luke told the counselor.

Luke told her. He didn't go to her to discuss his college options.

That means he must have discussed what they call "personal problems," the "and stuff" as Luke put it. Does this mean he doesn't need me anymore? He needs someone who can help him. But what has the counselor done? Nothing. Nothing has changed.

I refuse to let this go into the hands of a school

guidance counselor.

I understand that it must have taken a lot of guts to talk to Ms. Turner.

I want to say it's great he talked to her.

I want to know exactly what he told her.

I want to say he did the right thing.

Instead I talk about the graduation party. Suddenly it seems very important to have the best party in the class, in the history of Plains High. I can handle an invitation list and the menu. I can order Plains High School party napkins. I can make a party soundtrack. I can do these things.

–Maybe we should, like, have like non-Mexican food too, you know? For the party?

–Yeah, yeah, we could have some pizza or something, in case.

Truth:

I am mad at Luke because he talked to Ms. Turner. This truth disgusts me, but there it is in all its twisted glory. If he confided in her, am I still the keeper of his secret? Is the secret out? If she knows, will she make it right? I can't go to her and tell her what I know. That would violate my word.

I don't know how to make what he told me into something that I can live with.

I want to do the right thing. I want to be the right person.

I am jealous he talked to Ms. Turner. I should be relieved or grateful.

I am a horrible person. A crap friend.

I have done nothing. Nothing wrong to deserve my feelings of unworthiness. Nothing right to earn a feeling of self-worth. I am stuck being Rebecca, the friend who listens, nods her head, holds a hand, and allows her best friend to suffer. Allows Weston to exist in this rotten world.

I bite my hangnail, and it rips down my nail bed. I pick at the painful little edge.

I do not want to sit idle while Luke suffers and Weston goes free, yet I am incapable of making things right.

A single tiny pearl of blood next to my nail is pain.

I have the will but not the way out.

THE FOOD COURT

I agree to dress shop with Tiffany. Prom is April 6th, less than a month away. When we get to the mall, she tells me that she already has a dress. Now she needs shoes, pantyhose, et cetera. She wanted to come because she knew I didn't have a dress and she thought it would be fun to try on dresses together. Besides, she can return hers if she finds a better one. Her dress is gorgeous. There are several sizes available in the dress that she bought weeks ago. She decides to try it on for me. A soft yellow gauzy sheath that hugs her curves and creates tiny disturbances in the air behind her as she sashays between the racks.

–I should buy all these dresses and return them after the prom.

–That's genius, Tiff. Do it.

–I'm not sure the store would sell them all at once. You know, they might get suspicious.

I decide to play the prom-dress game. I don't have a date, yet. I could maneuver a few guys into asking me. So far I've put off the whole thing. I am not sitting by the phone, as they say. I'm not about to flat-out ask a guy either. So I am stuck. Probably I should secure the date first, then the dress. But the dress is more fun, I admit.

At first I go for Hollywood slink. I like how the style hangs on the rack. The dresses slip between my fingers as I run my hand down the material. On my body, they scream: Look at my breasts (good) and: see my ass jiggle (bad). Slink is not for me. Next I try the flounce. I don't like the way these look on the hanger. On my body, however, the dresses float around my hips and cinch my waist into a shape I hardly recognize as mine. Impressive.

A rainbow of gowns line my dressing room. I hang each silky-gauzy explosion back on its proper hanger after I have twirled around the floor and spun in front of the three-way mirror. Tiffany instructs me to rotate in full circles, right and then left, and I giddily rise up on my toes and oblige her. I hold a corner of my skirt, seeing myself descend a large marble staircase in a candlelit palace (cue the violins).

Of course, there are no Hollywood staircases in the dressing room. No chairs either. I miss the stairs, but chairs would only confuse this process: There is no way to sit in any of these dresses. The flowing fabric begs for graceful turns, for grand instrumental music. I wish I could waltz. When Tiff experiments with a Britney Spears hip thrust in a long peach strapless gown, we nearly die laughing at the bump and grind performed beneath layers of dense tulle.

Then. The light blue one with a tiny line of crystals across the bust and layers of tulle below the corseted waist. It is the one. I love it. A dress meant for me. Tiffany coos when I rush out and twirl in front of the mirror. We agree.

I return the dressing room to change into my saggy,

tired jeans. Tiff lured me here under false pretenses, no doubt about that. Yet her motivation was thoughtful and even kind. I am grateful. The dress was worth it. The zipper sticks.

A slight panic builds in my unsteady fingers.

–Here, Bec, let me unzip it before you tear it to shreds.

I unlatch the door and Tiffany slips in between the dress folds as I face the full-length mirror. Tiffany peers over my shoulder, her forehead crinkled in concern. Our eyes meet in the full-length mirror. I clutch the dress to my chest, worried Tiff will see my ratty bottom-of-the-drawer underwear. Next she'll insist that we have to go to the lingerie department to try on skimpy bras and shop for lace underwear.

Her hands are two ice cubes on my spine. I yelp and nearly drop my dress. She tugs at the zipper, but it won't budge. This is clearly my dress; it refuses to leave my body. She tugs at it, tells me to suck it up. My hands press my sides closer, knit my ribs together. Tiffany gives a mighty yank.

The severed threads give way with an undeniable death scream.

The rip stuns me and I forget to clutch the dress to my chest, causing the ruined dress to slide down my belly and puddle around my knees. Here we are: Rebecca and Tiffany, Tiffany and Rebecca staring at the naked me in the mirror. Seconds pass, only milliseconds, before I grab my T-shirt and cover my bra. I almost turn to face Tiffany, except I realize that my butt would then be in the mirror. I pretend to be okay with her seeing me hanging out of my dingy underwear. Relax, she says. It's nothing I don't have, she says. I smile at her, watching in the mirror as my cheeks flush, knowing that she sees right through my trying to play it cool.

The rip is minor; we can barely find where the stitches gave way to Tiff's grip.

I hadn't planned to buy it today, and I don't ask the sales lady to put it on hold. I'm sure I don't want a ripped dress.

Tiffany suggests a Diet Coke break. She needs the caffeine right now.

The Food Court has a bakery, a taco place, and a pizza place. The movie theater has an entrance. There is an arcade, where we had a total ski-ball war last summer. This kid named Rick was genius at it. He had thousands of tickets and redeemed them for a huge stuffed animal—a green horse that he used as target practice for his bb gun. There is a burger place and an Orange Julius too.

The fast-food places on the perimeter have an acre of patio furniture spread out in an arc where everyone takes their food and sits mixed up. We get our goods: Two Diet Cokes from the Orange Julius. We find a spot where we can survey the scene, see who comes and goes. This is the mall entrance where most kids get dropped off by parents. Kids who drive park there too. Not Tiffany. We parked at the other end of the mall; Tiff said it has better access to the stores. It must be uncool to park near the Food Court these days. Check. I'll park near the other end next time.

Tiffany is waving at Mark. He sees her and gives her a small wave.

He'll come over, for sure.

He pays for his Coke and fries and comes to our table. We hang out. Mark is cool. I have known him as long as I have known Tiffany and Luke, but somehow we never hung out. He is into paintball and who knows what else. At school he seemed like the quiet type. Turns out that he and Tiffany are in ceramics together this year. He took it to fill a fine-arts requirement, and Tiff has been helping him sand and glaze. Now they are painting. So they have plenty to chat about.

Suddenly, I sense that Mark might ask me to prom.

It is too weird that Tiffany lured me here and now. First the dress. Then she insisted on Diet Cokes. Insisted we sit in view of the main door. And then Mark just happens to be in the mall this afternoon on a perfectly good Saturday paintball afternoon. I go for a refill on my drink. (I ask for real Coke this time without Tiffany there to witness my sugar fix.)

When I come back to the table, Weston is there.

WHAT I COULD HAVE SAID

Move over, you're in my seat.

Weston, you look good. Have you heard from Lucy?

Wanna share some fries? Why did Lucy leave?

I heard there was a fight last summer at your lake house? What's the story?

Weston, I heard that you are going into the military?

Do you and Roger still hang out?

Stop talking to Tiffany.

What's your dad like? Does he shine his shoes on Sunday afternoon?

Instead I engage the doe eyes. I flip my hair with a carefully casual chin tilt as I lower myself into an empty seat next to Mark. I set the Coke on the table and sip from the straw as I observe the small talk start and stutter. Tiffany is flushed. Her eyes tighten ever so slightly at the corners as she leans her elbows on the table and smooths her hair with a flat palm. (This shows off her new French manicure.) The boys talk about school. Graduation. Never mention prom. Turns out, Weston asked Mark to meet him at the mall to see *Spider-man*.

–I have been *dying* to see that movie.

The four of us go to the theater. Mark offers to buy my ticket. I let him.

THE DINER

After the matinee we stumble into the eerie evening light. The boys hustle through the frigid breeze toward their car with Tiffany between them. They call out to me to hurry up. Mark is hungry again. It's suppertime. There is a brief debate about restaurants and available cash. Between the four of us we have about 20 dollars. Tiffany invites them to the diner, our treat, since they took us to the movies.

We drive separately. I ride next to Tiffany and respond to her chatter as if I am reading from a bad TV-movie script. I say, This is cool, but no pie, okay? She agrees and laughs. Relax, she says. Weston and Mike. I can't believe it, she says. It's just a bite to eat—aren't you hungry? They have salads you know, huge things with meat and cheese. No French fries, no pies, she says. Coffee, yes.

The diner is loud. It's suppertime and the weekend regulars have turned out. Grandparents in tow. Kids amuck. We wait 20 minutes for a booth near the back. The boys talk at Tiffany. I play it calm, hoping the bitch factor will keep me aloof so I don't get tricked up on some stupid thing I say.

I am not afraid of this Weston. This Weston here in the diner is not the Weston who did those things, I tell myself. But that doesn't make sense at all. Here I am near him, about to slide into a booth across from him. I just go with it. Ride the wave of chance or fate or destiny that put me in this diner with Weston. The lobby is crowded. I am careful not to brush his arm. Tiffany is between us. I lean on Mark when I laugh at my own jokes.

What if Luke comes to the diner and sees us here? My heart stops, then races. My cheeks go numb. I pick at the dry skin on my lip. I reach into my purse for Chapstick. I rub it across my lips. The tube slips from my hand and falls to the carpet. It rolls away beneath a forest of pant legs. I am desperate for it. Tiffany grabs my arm and holds me upright as I plunge after it. Rebecca, use mine, she laughs.

I keep my eyes glued to the large plate-glass windows that surround the foyer, looking for Luke or his car driving past.

Tiffany reads my mind: Luke is out of town, right? She asks me on the way to our booth. I pick flecks of sand and lint from the wax of my recovered Chapstick, a nice lady had fished it out from beneath her toddler's legs. It's true. He is out of town. I had completely blanked out on that. His parents took the family to visit relatives a good four hours away. He won't be back until late Sunday. He may even miss Monday morning at school. Luke is out of town. I am here with Tiffany, Mark, and Weston.

We order a Coke and French fries. Tiffany gets diet, of course.

Tiffany tells them how she loves this place and that we come here a lot to hang out. It will be sad, won't it? When we can't come here anymore, next year at this exact time we will all be somewhere else, she says in one breath. I hate that she spills her guts about the diner in front of Mark and Weston. They can't possibly appreciate this place the way that we do. Mark says he's going to KU. He hasn't gotten an acceptance, but he has decent grades and solid letters of rec. He's not sweating it, but he does worry about getting into the right dorm. Tiffany talks about Kansas Newman, her first choice. She'll get in; she hopes for a full ride scholarship. Weston talks about the navy.

It turns out that his dad, Principal Ames, was a bigshot navy guy. I vaguely knew Ames was in the military, but my dad never served. Ames travelled around the world and saw Naples, Italy and Paris, France and lived for a long time in Virginia. That was all before Weston was born, before his dad got out of the military and moved back here. This is my first question to Weston. "So, why did he move back to Kansas?" It was because of Weston's mom. Principal Ames moved here to marry Weston's mom. He got hired here to coach and teach. Weston says his dad wants to write a book about being in the navy. He writes on Sunday mornings.

When he talks about his dad, I put his dad and Principal Ames in the same body. I know that they are the same person. Except I can't imagine Ames at home in front of the TV. Mowing the lawn, scrubbing the toilet. I don't ask him about his mom. We were in the seventh grade when she died. I sent flowers. My mom helped me to pick out the arrangement—sunflowers and tiny purple flowers. I wrote a card: *My condolences, Rebecca White*. I looked up how to spell *condolences*. We went to the viewing and filed past the open coffin. My flowers bloomed just to the left of the whole scene.

In the reception line, I gave Weston a hug, shook his dad's hand. Loss naked in their slack faces, empty eyes. As I looked into their eyes—me as someone in the official line to give condolences gave me courage to look them in the eye—something simmered there, in both the son and the new widower. Weston's sallow skin was hot to the touch. When I hugged him, I pressed him to my chest and he leaned into me. His forearms met on my back. I watched him hug all the kids in our class. One at a time. It was the same devastating hug.

I wanted to do more for the motherless son, his father. My mom taught me how to make Grandma's salmon and pea casserole. We dropped it off midweek with a note explaining how to defrost and reheat it in the oven, covered in foil, at 350 degrees.

Their grief at the viewing, later at the funeral and burial, was all textbook. I had been to a funeral before for a distant aunt. I knew how things were supposed to happen. They would do what had to be done. Buck up. Shake hands, eat baked lasagnas and casseroles, and get on with it. Move on. Run a few miles. Get back to work. Study for the next geography quiz.

At the crowded funeral I sat near the back with my mom, who kept her arm draped over my shoulders. Tiffany sat next to me and we clutched hands. I admired Principal Ames and Weston, their ramrod backs and red-rimmed eyes. I thought that this was it: life's greatest sadness. The burden of being left behind. To bear up under the weight of being left behind was noble. I was sure they appreciated my flowers.

I bite my tongue. All these years later, I want to ask

Weston about those stupid sunflowers I sent. During his otherwise unrestrained comments tonight, he says nothing about his dead mother. He wants to talk about the navy, his future, and his life after graduation. The start of his real life. He doesn't think of life after graduation as the LAG. I don't dare make the joke in front of him.

Weston has already talked to the recruiters at school. They materialize in the school halls, looking sharp, and, as Ms. Walters would say, virile (a new vocabulary word). Their uniforms pressed, barely giving way at the knees and elbows. Their black dress heels shined. Weston has gone to their downtown offices and retaken the ASVAB, he says. His score was decent, he says. But he won't be touching anything electronic. His dad told him to look into the Air Force and the marines, except he is not interested. It is the navy for him. He has known since at least tenth grade, he says.

He plans to enlist as soon as he graduates. He'll think about college later. He wants to get it started. The basic training is killer, but he is hardcore ready. Shit is happening in this world. The War on Terror is hardcore. America is right there, you know? College can wait. It is not going anywhere. KU will be there when he's done getting it on in the ranks. He wants to see Afghanistan, China, Egypt, the Panama Canal, et cetera. The world.

His dad, you know, was a navy guy, bigtime.
By the end of the night, I am grateful. Sweet small-town happenstance. Tiffany didn't help me buy a prom dress, yet her good intentions led to Weston. We sat in a booth and he freely spoke. I know his dreams. His ambitions. These are what I can take from him. The price he will pay. I have the what. Now I need the how.

ACCEPTANCE LETTERS

Tuesday's homeroom tick lurches while we page through science books and novels. One kid highlights his chemistry book in alternate stripes of yellow and pink.

Mrs. Silverton banned talking. No study groups. We should use this valuable time to do homework. This is not recess. Et cetera.

Then the notes start. We scribble away while Mrs. Silverton, sure that we are doing our own busy-work, grades a stack of papers.

We write with purpose and fill pages at a time. There are soulful metaphors and school-inappropriate nouns, verbs, and adjectives.

Acceptance letters arrived from KU yesterday.

I felt the huge white packet and knew I was accepted. I took the mail in the kitchen, dropped my bag, and set the packet down. The thick white envelope with the official university stamp perched there in the middle of the empty round table. It pulsed. I backed away, kicked off my sandals. I went to pee.

When I came back to the kitchen I washed my hands

with soap up the elbows, scrubbed my nails with the vegetable brush. I rinsed my hands and then pulled a fresh towel from the kitchen drawer. I rubbed the skin dry until hands turned an angry red. So I took down the lotion from above the kitchen sink where my mom keeps it. I pushed it into my skin in little circular motions.

I wiped my hands on my jeans.

I slid my finger under the flap and ripped it open. I got in. My essay did the trick. Thank you, Mother Jones.

I raced through the dormitory pamphlets (assignments would be made at a later date) and endless forms. No scholarship.

Homeroom today is thick with suppressed energy. I didn't want to ask Tiffany or anyone else. There's no reason to ask Luke. He still hasn't applied.

Then this kid, John, showed up with a message for Mrs. Silverton and on his way out the door he slipped me Tiffany's note. She got in. She says to relax about the scholarship. Her mom called KU this morning, the award letters are sent later in the spring.

I lean back in my desk, prop my feet up. She sent me the note before I had even thought that she might have more information about the scholarships. She read my mind. Way to go, Tiffany.

I write a note to Jackie, she of the ever-slouched spine, and tell her what Tiffany said about the scholarships. She writes back that she is sure I will get a full ride. No doubt.

INTERVIEW

Mrs. Buckley scheduled an appointment on Thursday, mid-March, during my homeroom period to interview Ames for Personal Personnel Profiles. I check in with Mrs. Silverton in homeroom, show her my pass. My supplies are prepared: spiral notebook and Bic pens. I review my list of questions as I walk down Senior Hall toward the Main Office. I am a reporter doing research for the school paper.

Mrs. Buckley waves me behind her desk. She nods into a phone and stacks a pile of blue forms. Finally, she hangs up and makes small talk about the school assembly, graduation, et cetera. She tells me Mr. Ames is running late and I should take a seat, he'll be right with me.

The clock lurches along, but I am not tired. I review my questions again. I want to flee, except I can't think of a legitimate excuse. It is now or never, I say to myself and steel my nerves.

He opens the door and tells me to come inside, come inside.

His office is bigger than I remembered from my visit

sophomore year when he informed me about my soon-to-be-rectified grade in gym. Spring air floods through the window, ruffles the blinds. The shelves are lined with binders and books. The walls have framed diplomas and awards granted by the U.S. Navy. There are no pictures on his desk. His coffee cup is balanced on a stack of papers. His email is open, the inbox filled with unopened letters. I sit and face him. I set my spiral on my lap, uncap my Bic, and thank him for giving me the interview.

His eyes range over my features, trying to place me. He has seen me in the halls. He held my elbow when I swooned last week. It clicks in his head: Rebecca White, good kid. Responsible. Tall. Quiet. He mentally ticks off these attributes as he drums his fingers on the desktop.

I want to ask him about his dead wife. I want to ask him about his son.

I ask him if I may tape the interview, and he says okay.

I start with my list: Where did he go to high school? (Plains High. I already knew this, but I thought it was a good beginning.) He tells me about the school back in his day. There were only a few hundred students back then. Mr. Phelps was the choir director back then too. Ames played sports: basketball (forward) and football (linebacker). He was prom king along with Sally Jeffers, who is now a lawyer here in town.

"Could you talk about your military experience?" He tells me he enlisted right after high school.

"The Navy was my first choice. Just like my Uncle Tim. He served and I always knew I wanted to do the same for my country."

I want to ask about Weston's mom next. It follows in chronological order.

Instead I ask him how he became a principal. He went to college after the navy. He was a social studies teacher for years. "I loved teaching, I did." As a coach, he learned how to get things done. "Kids have got to want it; have the passion." When students have a passion for something, they can accomplish great things. "I pushed my athletes, two-a-days whenever possible. High expectations are key. If you expect the best, you can get the goods out of people who may not know their own strength." I scrawl that down as he watches.

He looks at the clock.

I continue down my list of questions, telling him that these are the same questions I plan to ask all participants in the series. (I plan to do a series, even though I don't have any other interviews lined up yet.)

"If you had one book on a deserted island, what book would you choose?"

"The Bible. It has everything: stories, lessons, heck, even poetry in the psalms, the Song of Songs."

"What music do you have in your car or home stereo right now?"

He listens to the radio.

"Steak or fish?"

With a hungry look in his eyes, "Steak."

He glances at the clock for the second time.

"If you had to pick the three values that are the most important to you, what would they be?"

"Hard work. Integrity. Victory."

"Winning," he says, "is the goal. No matter if it is a basketball game, a research paper, a science experiment or, heck, trying to land a good job." Being the best is the goal.

And there he sits, Principal of the School. Proof of his convictions.

He glances at his watch.

I thank him and gather my things. I fumble with my notebook and stuff it into my bag. I am about to shake his hand when Mrs. Buckley opens the office door. She pokes her head in and says that Jill Turner from guidance is here to see him. He smiles and leans back in his chair. I look at him. He does not look like Principal Ames ready to see guidance counselor Ms. Turner. He is a man waiting for Jill, the young Ms. Turner, to visit his office in the middle of the day, with no appointment. I pass her on my way out. Her heels pitter-patter past me as she calls out her good mornings. The air ripples behind her; her sweet perfume settles on my skin.

The interview was a bust. I am exhausted. I can smell the sweat in my armpits. I stop in the hall and look at my notes. Pathetic. I could have asked him about having his son in the same school. Then he would have talked about Weston, at least. Somehow I thought getting near him would be enough. Would be magically effective. Would tell me something I need to know.

I am treading water, my legs hot with pain and heavy.

I thought Ames would look at me and know there was something wrong. I wanted him to see in my eyes the truth about Weston and I wanted him to fix what his son had done. These incoherent desires take shape in my mind only because they are left unfulfilled. I didn't know what I wanted, but, now that I didn't get it, now I can tell you.

Now I know: I wanted him to know more than I did. I wanted him to be the grownup.

All I have learned is that Ms. Turner is friendly with Principal Ames. They were happy to see each other, despite the workday. Her perfume was freshly applied. The scent went straight to my brain.

DEAR ME

It is the Friday before Spring Break. I apply a pinprick of perfume to my inner wrist, left then right. It is my mother's *Obsession*, borrowed from her bathroom cabinet. I put the jar back in its place before I leave for school.

The halls have thinned out. Parents pull their kids out early to squeeze in another day at Disney World. Some kids take the day off and chalk it up to senioritis. The halls are not deserted, however, because tonight is the girls' basketball sectionals. The players wear their team T-shirts for game day spirit and courage. They rehearse plays in their heads and try to keep a lid on their nerves.

My mom and I have no plans for break. She will work as usual. I will hang around the house, perfecting the art of doing nothing. I'll make chocolate chip cookies, watch too much daytime TV, and convince myself to clean under my bed, perhaps.

I didn't make plans with Tiffany or Luke to go on a trip. Luke's family can't muster the cash. Tiff says she has to spend most of break finishing a ceramics project and working out for prom. She joined a health club.

English class is the last place we want to be. Ms. Walters distributes plain white paper and legal envelopes. She told us last time that our homework was to bring a pen and one stamp. A good half of the class forgot the stamp. This deflates her bursty energy, yet she doesn't give up on her assignment.

Ms. Walters and I struck a truce. I got my act together after Christmas Break and showed her my Mother Jones essay. She wasn't able to inch up my A-, which would've been nice. Really I just wanted to show it to her. I wanted to show her I had lined up my margins and used a judicious font. She was glad I had finished it. "What a relief, Rebecca."

Ms. Walters tells us we will write a letter today in class. I take this assignment seriously, not giving into the senior spring blow-off temptation. My clean sheet of paper and a fresh envelope are centered on my desk. I place the envelope flush against its side. I wait for instructions. She explains the rules.

She will not read the letters.

We will seal the envelopes, address, and stamp them.

We should address them to our permanent address.

She will mail them in five years.

She tells us to brainstorm first or free write.

She takes a letter from her desk. It is the letter she wrote to herself when she was a senior in high school. She reads it out loud to us. The letter from the teenage Ms. Walters is sweet. It's filled with I wants, I dreams, I hopes, et cetera. This letter is a letter in a bottle cast out to sea. This message, however, is guaranteed to return to us. Our youthful handwriting will be preserved. Our younger selves captured on a page. I like the idea.

She reassures us she won't read our letters. We should write about where we want to be in five years. Or we should write about where we are right now. We can describe our bedroom or our favorite place. We can list our favorite songs and movies. We can talk about the important people in our lives. We should aim for five paragraphs. She will check off our names on her list when we hand them in. Twenty-five points, just like that.

Kids groan and laugh with nerves. We have the rest of the hour to work. I already need more time. She says we have the hour but no longer. She doesn't want us to discuss it or to think about it too much. She wants us to capture our ideas and feelings as they are, right now, today, at this moment. Go.

Tiffany bends over her desk. She traces the edge of her empty page with her long nails. What will she write? Luke is in school today and will have Ms. Walters next hour. What will he write? I'll give him one of my extra stamps during passing period.

I brainstorm, make notes, even outline. I write it out. Writing to myself. Using the past tense. It is maddening.

Dear Rebecca,

You were accepted to Kansas University.

~~When you were a little girl you dreamed about horses. Black stallions galloped through wheat fields and jumped rickety fences, clearing rusty barbed wire by inches. When you were a senior in high school you stopped dreaming about horses. You watched men dressed for business jump from the towers to save their lives. The horses never~~

~~returned to your dreams. Instead you tried to dream about merry-go-rounds and picnics. You dreamed that one day you walked on a beach with Luke. It was his first time to see the ocean. Together under the sun he gathered sea glass to fill your pockets. You were happy.~~

I ask for a blank sheet. In the last five minutes I fill the fresh page as fast as I can without letting my brain slow me down or bother to check my spelling. A free write freely written and quickly forgotten. I lick the envelope flap and press it down. The taste of glue tingles my tongue with the taste of elementary school.

Writing to myself was an hour in another world. It was being alive for one glorious hour five years in my future, five years beyond this present mess. I can't get there soon enough. I have to believe I will get there.

MARCH MADNESS

I passed Luke a stamp between classes, hoping that he too would write his letter, wondering what he would say to himself.

Later that same afternoon I leave school early. The girls' basketball team made it to State for the first time in the school's history. As the newspaper's senior photographer, I ride with the team. The girls are pulled thin. They plod and prance by as they climb into the bus with overstuffed gym bags, their hair stretched back in tight ponytails or woven into thick braids. Cynthia, the hard-court star with a killer three-point shot, clutches a matted blue elephant. A plush zoo boards the old bus: pink bears, puppy dogs with sad eyes, even a plastic quarter house figurine. I open the school camera case and check for the tripod, batteries, and the zoom lens. I know all my equipment should be stowed, except I don't want to miss a shot. These girls are razor tough. Win or lose, this is history in the making for each one of them. For Plains High. And I am in the thick of it.

This will be the last game I shoot. The boys lost in the

first round. Underclassmen have already signed up for the spring track and tennis pictures. I hope the girls win tonight, for their sake and mine. This is one of the growing number of *lasts*, before we take that stilted graduation walk and have our parties, and head into the long summer before college. (College looms with a capital C.)

Extra-stuffed gym bags and pillows in a rainbow of pastel colors (snatched warm this morning from each girl's bedroom) crowd the bus. I take some candid shots, which might look great on a victory page, if there is one. Braids and ponytails orbit their smiles.

When we pull out of the school lot, another bus, rented by the booster club, follows. Parents trail the second bus in a parade of minivans. They honk their horns and wave victory fingers from unrolled windows. I get goose bumps.

At the game, I run the sidelines. I climb the bleachers for a bird's-eye angle. The fans are bright-eyed parents, bored siblings, and compliant grandparents. The cheerleaders make sustainable noise; get the crowd in synch to chant our school letters: P-H-S clap. P-H-S clap. P-H-S clap.

We lead 32-26 at half-time. I head to the snack bar in the school's cafeteria for nachos. Some seniors pull up folding chairs around a lunch table. Of course there is game chatter: Cynthia sank four amazing three pointers, but has three fouls. Coach Lyndell kept a cool head and mouth all during the first half—even when the ref missed a few calls that cost us. My nachos deep are thick with cheese goo and jalapeños.

Tiffany and Mark walk into the snack bar. I didn't know she planned to come. We go half-cheeks on the chair while Mark looks for extra chairs. I didn't know she planned to come with Mark. He wanders off to get food. She looks at me, raises her eyebrows at my scrunched brow. It turns out that she and Mark rode together with his mom. Mark's sister plays point guard. She sits the bench. She is just a freshman; great things are still to come for her beneath the hoop.

Tiffany suggests a powder-room break and I follow her.

Pepto-Bismol pink tiles line the bathroom walls. She pulls me into a stall, locks the door, and we lean against the cold metal. She grabs my hands and dances, tossing her hair back and forth over her head in wild arcs.

–He asked me!

Mark asked her to prom. She tells me the whole story. After we went to the movies that time with Weston, Mark found her in the halls after school, and they had small-talked for 20 minutes. Then he called her a few days later. Came by her house, and they took a walk around the neighborhood. (I knew all this. He had called me first; after all, he had paid for my movie ticket. We didn't have much to say to one another. I called him back once. Found myself talking about Tiffany, how great she is and all. And now. Figures. It worked out for Tiffany, and that counts for something.) Then, late last night on the phone, he asked her if she had a prom date. She spazzed, but kept her voice smooth to tell him she didn't. She totally had planned to go with Steve, but that hadn't been official or anything.

She just knows that he can get a butter-cream cummerbund to match her dress. And his skin is just made for that color. It will make his eyes so crazy blue.

I am happy for her, which feels good.

I hug her, and we giggle, shriek, and the noise smacks

into the metal stalls and shimmers over the pink tiles. I swear not to tell anyone yet. She wants to break the news herself. She thinks that so-and-such will be jealous, et cetera. I lift the camera to my eye and snap her wide-open eyes and teeth shined by triumph. A dress and a date. And it is a real "date" too. She and Mark are not yet really but pretty close to actually dating now. This is the best possible way to go to prom.

I shoot the rest of the game. We win.

We rush the floor, mill around and high-five the players. The coach shakes my hand, along with just about everyone else's. Tiffany and I bump into one another, literally. She has Mark in tow; she clutches his hand. He stands close behind her; they interlace their fingers. Principal Ames walks by and quickly shakes my hand, slaps me on the back. Ames mentions that he looks forward to my Personal Personnel Profile, "that article," about him in the next edition. I say it will be ready soon and avert my eyes. I stare at my untied shoelace.

When I shuffle over to the bleacher to sit down and tie it, the crowd towers over me. When I finish, the gym is half-empty. The crowds move fast toward the fan bus and mini-vans. Our hometown is still a tedious bus ride away. But first there will be hours spent at an overcrowded pizza place, slices of pepperoni to inhale, and pitchers of Coke to imbibe.

Bathroom break. I pee. In the grimy bathroom mirror I see a distinct mustard yellow-orange smudge on my chin. Great. I pick at the dried nacho cheese. When I head to the bus, there is a cluster of people near the wide-open gym door. Cold air presses their hands to coat collars. The spring air tonight is more like the shock of the first cold autumn days, when you are caught with only a jacket. Principal Ames is there.

Then I see Weston, hands shoved in his pockets. He stands with his neck stretched to one side, his chin tilted across the room as if to make it clear that he will not look you straight in the eye.

My skin prickles hard and my stomach tightens.

Ames talks to Ms. Turner, from guidance. She has her legs planted wide, her hip pressed out by a curve in her lower spine. She looks young. She looks maternal. As I squeeze in between Ames and Ms. Turner, she reaches up and tugs at her hair. Weston does not look at me. He makes a point of looking at the opposite end of the gym. His shoulders are bunched up around his ears. He is tension personified.

The night air is sharp, wet against my skin. I sink into my seat on the bus and gather my camera gear like a fortress around me.

I replay the scene in my head.

Ames, Weston, Ms. Turner.

Of course.

Principal Ames is allowed to date. His wife died years ago.

Ms. Turner is not married.

If I were Weston, I wouldn't make eye contact with Ms. Turner either.

I breathe easy. Weston wasn't rigid with impatience and anger just because I, Rebecca White, walked by. Weston didn't see me. He couldn't see me, not really. Weston had his fists balled up, jammed deep in his pockets at Ms. Turner or his dad or maybe it was just the way she tugged at her hair, the way Ames had loosened his tie.

SPRING BREAK

An entire week: a respite from the crowded school halls. It should be a vacation, a break, a chance to forget school. But there is one thing on my mind: The Party. The spring break party will be at Weston's lake house. I intend to be there.

Sophomore year Tiffany had to drag me along. I watched the kids, how they drank in hurried gulps and laughed at baseball. That was the night I saw Lucy wrapped around Weston's waist. The memory burns. Lucy, who has not been seen or heard from since her family left town. This year I plan to drag Tiffany there. I can't go alone.

Saturday, I sleep late and then bliss out on the couch all afternoon. The haze of vacation ends Sunday evening when I ask my mom about Lucy's family. Mom and I were eating dinner, the radio talk show turned loud enough to cover the silent spots between bites. I thought she might know what had happened to the Robinson family. Maybe her dad lost his job. Maybe they won the lottery. Whatever. When I ask about Lucy's family, mom seals her lips around her fork. She forces potatoes back and down. She extracts a clean fork.

–Strange you ask, we were just talking about the Robinsons at work.

(Pause. I chew my chicken.)

–How long since they moved now?

I tell her that Lucy left school when were juniors. About a year ago, more or less. I tell her that I hadn't known Lucy, except I saw her around school, of course, and at a party once sophomore year.

Mom puts her fork down and reaches for the corn. There are frown lines around her mouth. Her forehead is creased as she picks and arranges her words.

–Was Lucy popular with the boys? Well, it is just I heard she got herself into trouble.

This is my mother's way of saying one of many things: *she got pregnant* being only one. Maybe she thinks they had sex or just that Lucy somehow let things go too far (whatever "too far" means in my mom's head is hard to measure.)

I don't go into specifics about what she may think "trouble" with a boy means. Instead my questions gather in the back of my throat. I can hardly believe that "trouble with a boy" would be enough for the entire family to up and flee.

–So, what, the whole family left town?

Mom piles a rounded spoon of corn on her plate. She salts it with two quick shakes.

–Oh Becca, I don't have all the details and I shouldn't gossip, but it seemed like something was not quite right about *that* girl.

–What? What was wrong with Lucy? And who was the boy?

–Well, just stay out of that kind of trouble. You are such a good girl, with good judgment. You're going places if you can stay on the right track.

It was a fine speech. She wants to run her fingers through my hair and give me a reassuring pat on the shoulder. I sit up, lock my shoes in a vise beneath my seat.

I want to know more. She slides her plate away with a shove, even though it is half-filled with meat and corn. She goes to the fridge and returns with a tub of ice cream and the chocolate sauce.

I work my way across my plate, one bite of starch or meat at a time. My mom doesn't want me to ask her anything more; thus, there must be more. She never eats ice cream until after the dishes are finished. She has a few scoops after the dishes are stowed in the dishwasher, in her pajamas and robe, in front of the TV news. Often we both grab a huge slab of vanilla and cover it with nuts and fruit and chocolate. Now here she is eating her vanilla with the half-eaten meal still on the table.

–So, that's it. You won't tell me anything.

–Becca, calm down, honey. It was a long day. Please don't use that tone of voice with me, especially when I'm exhausted.

I am tired of her being tired and tired of trying to negotiate the silence between each bite. I do something novel: I tell her, Fine, whatever, I'm going to Dad's. She sits at the kitchen table, a spoon in her hand, and looks concerned and miffed at the same time.

I grab my jacket and storm through the kitchen, my purse slung over my shoulder and my car keys in hand.

She stands in front of the door.

–What's going on with you Rebecca? Why are you so angry? Talk to me. Please. Be civil.

I roll my eyes. We stand. The tub of vanilla has started to sag. It will thaw and be no good. I hate her for that too.

I don't go to my dad's place. I drive to Tiffany's house. Mark, prom-date Mark, is there and they were watching a movie. I tell Tiff, and Mark, that I had another fight with my mom. She is seated next to Mark on the couch. They've turned off the movie, but stayed deep in the couch grooves, their thighs melded. Tiffany reaches out a hand and rubs my knee as I explain why my mom is so terrible. I sound ridiculous even to my own ears. I explain how she said what she said, the way her words didn't match her facial expressions. How she took the corn, salted it, but didn't even eat it. I sound wacked out. Tricked up by my own inarticulate tongue. Tiffany should tell me I am not crazy, that my mom doesn't understand me. She should get off the couch and hug me. I did not want to cry. Mark looks baffled. He goes to get a Coke from the upstairs fridge. Tiffany slides over to my couch and hugs me, finally.

–Becca, can I make it all better?

Rebecca Before wanted to drink coffee and drive a green jeep. She wanted to hang out at the diner and eat plates and plates of French fries. She wanted to share an entire peanut butter pie with Tiffany and Luke. She wanted to be in college and afraid of the communal shower germs. She wanted to be 25, married with a career and a baby on the way. So many wants. I wanted.

Rebecca Before wanted to have a good time the way good kids are supposed to deserve. Now I want to shed Luke's hold on me. I want to forget Lucy.

The word *want* starts to sound ridiculous in my head. What a strange word: *want*. It just sounds wrong, like a duck: want, want, want-want. A duck want-wants. I can't get my mind around all the ways I want Tiffany to make it all better.

I make her promise to go with me to Weston's lake house for the party. At first she perks up at the idea. I knew that she wanted to go, but she had not yet figured out how. Then I ruin it for her: I make her promise that it would be just the two of us. Mark has to do something else that night. I need it to be just girls. I want it to be like sophomore year, that night under the stars the time we stayed out late and watched her sprinklers come to life at three a.m. in front of her house.

She agrees, even though she doesn't like it. What will Mark think?

I blow my nose for the thousandth time on toilet paper. I know she can make him see how her poor Rebecca needs her.

Mark comes back with three Cokes, but I tell him no thanks.

I leave them to make out like the two ravenous young things they are. Tiffany will mad-kiss him (like a girl wanting more than she knows how to ask for) so that she can ditch him to go with me to Weston's party.

I drive home and then blast music while I take a hot shower. My mom doesn't hear a thing, deep asleep in dreams she never tells me.

I got close to Principal Ames and asked all the wrong questions. Now I will get close to Weston. At his own party.

Weston: the knife against my throat instead of Luke's. Weston's dick throb-hard. Fine, I can't cut it off, I admit that. But. I know the truth. I can use the truth against him slick as a knife wet with blood. I know what he did. I know he wants to be a man. I know he wants to serve his country and strut his navy uniform in ports around the globe. I have the truth; it will jail Weston. I don't have to break my promise to Luke: I won't tell a soul who doesn't already know.

CAN'T STOP

The next morning Luke drops by the house with this girl, Jennifer. He met her at the KanMart drugstore the day before. His mom sent him to buy baby aspirin and toothpaste. Jennifer runs the cash register at the front—scans barcodes and makes exact change for impatient customers. Yesterday they were shorthanded, so the manager assigned her to stock the new shipment of toothpaste.

She must be a few years out of high school. Her nails are purple claws. Her hair is white blond, hangs to her waist in waves of hydrogen peroxide. Her tight jeans make my own crotch itch. They ride up her ass and sit low on her waist. Surely this is not the measure of modern engineering.

I'm still in my pajamas when they ring the bell. We go into the kitchen and make toast, one of my specialties. They talk at me about the movie they saw last night, *Solaris*. Of course it was science fiction and she is a big fan. Now Luke is too. Apparently, she converted him to time-space warps.

I spread butter on my charred toast. Sprinkle the cinnamon-and-sugar. Slide another slice into the toaster. They don't touch the toast. Her hands flutter about her face, alight on her shoulders, reach under the table toward Luke's thigh (I imagine). She goes to the bathroom.

I stare at Luke, who gushes about Jenni. She spells her name with an *i* and when he saw "Jenni" on her nametag at KanMart, he asked her about it. They were next to the toothpaste display. Luke is glad that she chooses to spell it with just one *i* instead of the more conventional *ie* or plain *y*. Ah, Jenni, he says.

Please.

I play it calm. I tuck my feet under my ass and lean my elbows on the table. I eat my toast and nod my head at him. He can't stop this love-gush for a girl he just met. A girl who is not a girl, but a drugstore-working girl-woman.

He has never liked a girl like Jennifer—Jenni—before. I am not worried about his liking her. She is a joke. He can't take her seriously for too long. This is some kind of magical-KanMart hookup for novelty's sake.

That evening Mom is at some meeting for her firm. She left pizza money—a sure sign she will be late and feels bad about it. I ordered a pepperoni with pineapple. Monday Night Football is on. I was about to reach for another slice when the doorbell rings and scares me senseless.

Stomach acids spin out of control and a serious case of indigestion bubbles. My heart drops, and then sticks in my throat. When I ask, "Who's there?" I hear Luke's voice and relax. He is alone.

As I let him in. I slap him on the shoulder (well, more like a wallop) to punish him for scaring me like that.

He eats some pizza. We watch TV. I eat more pizza.

I turn off the TV when the news starts.

We eat another slice.

I do not ask him about Jenni. He does not talk about her.

I ask him how he is doing, since.

I can smell his pepperoni breath from across the couch. Finally, he just talks about it. Once he starts, he can't stop.

He tells me he is better. He avoids Weston. Weston avoids him. Luke tells me that he is sad now. He feels like an idiot for thinking that Weston could want to be his friend. He hates that he went there in the first place. He is okay, okay? Just sad and sometimes mad too. He thanks me again and again for being his Becca, keeping his secret.

I tell him it is time to talk to someone.

–I did, Becca. I did.

He talked to the school counselor, Ms. Turner. He told Ms. Turner that he thinks he might be "gay." He thinks he *likes* guys and that his family will shun him for it. (So, he told her that much.)

He didn't tell Ms. Turner about Weston. He said that it didn't seem to matter anyway. How could he say it? If he told her, shit would happen. The whole world would crucify him.

He says that he thinks of Weston now, like, he can't stop thinking about him—what happened and more like wondering what he is doing right now. You know, imagining that they could still "resolve things" somehow. At night he thinks about trying to make it right with him. It's crazy talk. Tricked up in his head. There he is, Weston, in his head. What can Luke do?

After all these months, Luke doesn't want to remember Weston's face that night, just the way he grabbed him when he jerked him out of the car. He knows that Roger drove him back to his house. They had Luke in the middle seat. When Roger pulled up in front of his house, Weston jumped out the door and pulled Luke out of the cab. A tight grip on his forearm, the pressure of his fingertips. Weston said, "All you fags know what happens if you open your mouth, so keep your cocksucker shut." Luke stood there while they drove off. He went inside the house, snuck into the bathroom and cleaned up real good.

–I told myself then, my mouth is sealed tight. For good.

I continue to look him in the face, even though he can't look me in the eyes.

–Except, I told you Rebecca, I know. I was scared. Now I can't stop thinking of how Weston held me down—my arms clenched in his two hands—to let Roger pour the vodka. Why can't I stop that, feeling his hands on me? That is just wrong, you know? It has to stop. I have to get it together, you know?

–What Weston did is wrong.

–I just want to forget, you know?

–Luke, I won't tell. But, Luke, what if he does it to someone else? Have you thought about that? This world is too tricked up if Weston gets away with this. You don't deserve what he did to you, what he still does to you. Even though you say you want to forget, you can't.

I can't shut up now that Luke is here next to me and Weston is between us.

–That worthless shit gets away with being a jerk because we all kiss his ass—daddy's boy, heading to the navy. A Somebody. A hero, for god's sake. Can you live with that? Weston will be a hero, home with medals and stories about defending the seas or whatever.

He hits the refrain I loathe to hear:

–Rebecca, promise: don't tell. Please.

And, as a friend, I promise:

–I won't tell.

And then a mean rush of emotions, direct from my gut:

–Don't be surprised when Weston takes someone else down—another victim—since you are such a coward. Walk away. Walk away. Fuck Jenni. See if I care.

We stand in the empty living room. The TV is dark and silent. The house buzzes with my delirious anger. Luke reaches for my hand. I let him take it. I can't help it. He doesn't cry. Instead he takes my other hand. He feels a million miles away from me now. He is Luke from grade school. He is Luke from the diner. I tell him he better go. My mom will be home soon.

–Jenni doesn't know, okay?

That night I don't sleep. I don't even toss and turn. I lie flat on my back and decide how I will make Weston pay. I wanted it to go away. I wanted Luke to come to his senses, realize what had to be done. Or I wanted Luke to get over it. I wanted Weston to show he understood his crime. I wanted my mom to tell me it was none of my business. I wanted to graduate from high school and drive a green jeep.

I still have my mother's old sedan. And I still hate coffee.

At the party I will tell Weston what I know. A confrontation. I want him to know that I hate him. He deserves to know that I know. Maybe a part of him will feel shame. I want him to know that I am watching him.

He can't hurt me any more than knowing Luke's story already has.

TAINT: A STORY PROBLEM

Male/male rape exists. Men do not report it. If they report it, they are perceived to be gay. As a man, having people think you are gay (whether true or not) is worse than being raped. Rapes continue. The problem: the fear of being gay. The solution?

If A is raped by B, and both A and B are male, then both A and B must be gay. Is Weston gay? Does he hate gays? If A reports the crime, and P (where P = Public) believes him, and B is punished, is justice done when A is sentenced in parallel to a life tainted as *that gay kid who got raped*? B rapes A. A accuses B. A is innocent yet tainted. B may or may not be found guilty. If not, he is not tainted and goes free. If found guilty, B is tainted and the taint serves him well if placed in prison, where the taint may increase his status—make him the predator instead of the prey.

A was raped. It was wrong. B is guilty. A will not tell. The right thing is to have B convicted. B should pay for his crime, even if A cannot afford the price. What is the solution?

Luke is silenced. Silence is toxic. Silence is suffering.

B is free. B is guilty. B may do it again.
What is the solution?
Enter R.
B raped A. A is silent. Enter R.

CHAPTER FIVE

THE LAKE HOUSE

I go to the mall and buy a halter top that would freak my mother, but I will be sure she doesn't see it. It shows the tops of my breasts and the curve of air between. Even I can't stop staring at them in the dressing room mirror. Standing there in the full-length mirror, I see Luke holding my hands and begging me to let the whole thing go. But I shake my head and clear out his crazy denials. He doesn't know what is good for him. The barely-there shirt alone is enough to turn heads, but I go all out and buy the kind of jeans that hug my curves, and new summer sandals. I will freeze at the lake house. I count on it.

When Tiffany picks me up, she goes gaga over my new look. I slide into the passenger seat and reveal my new halter top from beneath my jacket. She makes a mock-shock face and reaches out to touch a breast with one accusatory finger. She covers her mouth and laughs. The car pulls away from the curb, and she jerks us left and right with her unsteady hands. I reach over and hold the steering wheel as she succumbs to the hilarity of me, Rebecca, showing off my cleavage.

It is a solid 30-minute drive to the lake house. After we leave the clusters of houses on the city's edge, the drive seems eternal. The fields stretch out between the grid roads. The one-mile span between each intersection feels like ten country miles. As we make a left turn onto yet another dirt road, I catch myself sitting with my shoulders hunched forward. My spine presses into the seat and the girls stand out. I need to practice before we get to the party. Get my game on. The plan: flirt with Weston, confront him with my bared cleavage, and make him confess; belittle him, then walk away with my head held high.

We have the radio set to the pop station, blaring top-40 hits to the thrill of our accelerated heart rates. Tiffany talks (and talks) about Mark this, Mark that, Mark this. She tells me that he found the exact right cummerbund, the ever-elusive shade of yellow that is neither too brassy nor too pale. Creamy butter, she calls it. Delicious. She made sure that Mark ordered the elegant white rose corsage for her wrist. I still don't have a date. Or a prom dress. Whatever. She avoids asking me about my prom plans. She relies on my resourcefulness and thinks that I will make it happen at the last minute. (Prom is one week from tonight.) She talks about Mark's friend, Jeremy, from the next town over. He has a car—something rugged, like a jeep—and he is nice enough. I feign interest, ask about his friends. No, I *am* interested and ask for details and gossip about this Jeremy to fill the time. Who knows?

Foot in door, beer in hand.

The place is packed with kids from school. We exchange a few smiles and waves. There are more boys than girls, I notice. Retro-80's pop music lures Tiffany toward a cluster of girls next to the stereo. I bet they are deep into planning a music-coup. Soon we will be immersed chest deep in the techno throb of house music.

I see Weston. He is wild with talk. He wipes his blond hair from his eyes with his palm. He sees me eyeing the gang of kids in his corner and offers me a beer even though I already have a half-filled bottle in my hand. I walk right up to him with a wry grin. It is time to get this contest started. Flirt, confront, belittle, and degrade.

–What about the funnel? I ask.

Weston catches my wrist in his fist and steadies his balance. We sway there. I resolve myself to his touch. I want to pry his fingers off my body. But I don't.

–Okay, this girl means business.

He is impressed by my funnel request and jazzed at the arrival of fresh meat for his legendary party game. He drags me into the next room, where hunting rifles and antlers adorn the walls above the bar. He tells me, Relax. He slurs it. He is out of his mind drunk. I am in control.

I hike up my jeans and balance on a barstool. I lean on the wooden bar, my head at an angle. I tell him that I heard all about funnels from some college friends at KU when I stayed in the dorms for a college visit last year. (This is a white lie, of course. Luke told me about the funnel. He told me about the feel of Weston holding his arms and the sear of the vodka down this throat.) I tell Weston that I don't get why it's so great. (I run my free hand through my hair, twisting a lock around my finger.) He promises to show me "how it's done."

A small crowd gathers. Some kid slaps Weston on the back and congratulates him on the NROTC scholarship. This is news to me. Then everyone is talking about

Weston's college plans and Weston decided not to enlist after all. NROTC will pay his way through the college of his choice. His dad made sure he applied months ago, proofread his essay, and drove him to the interview. *I am the son of a marine* is enough of a thesis statement to get a four-year deal. He got the acceptance letter earlier this week, and it is time to celebrate. Tiffany stands next to me as Weston announces to the room-at-large that he will go to KU on NROTC scholarship. Glasses are raised in his honor. A quick count reveals that more than half of us are KU bound in the fall. The room is thick with Jayhawk red, blue, and a streak of yellow.

Right here and now, he says, it's time for the funnel and these girls (meaning Tiffany and me) need a how-to lesson. There is the dirty white plastic funnel, unwashed by the looks of it. My brain sees a horrible medical procedure from a Nazi death camp. Torture. To which I am about to submit my bowels and my wits, and not necessarily in that order.

Check your dignity at the door. Done.

I take the plastic funnel between my lips and let tasteless vodka burn past my teeth and rip past my lungs. I gasp and sputter when it splashes into my gut. Vodka runs over my chin and down my chest. Wet stains blossom on the pale blue cotton of my new halter.

Tiff has better luck. She manages to make a good show of it. After we girls finish our turn, Tiffany takes me out onto the porch. She pulls my hand and we fumble with the screen door before we can emerge from the noise into the night air. We stand there wrapped in each other's arms.

She tells me not to be mad. I'm not mad, of course. I have no idea what she is talking about. She had to tell Mark it was okay. Don't worry, she says, she promises she will still take me home whenever I am ready. She swears.

Mark is here. He came with a bunch of guys. I lose Tiffany to him. She kisses my cheek and he pulls her to his chest. They go for a walk near the shore.

I stand in the lake air, blazed orange and pink by the setting sun—a giant orange and pink cummerbund across the sky. I grip the porch railing and watch the water move against the failing light. Weston has a full-ride scholarship to KU, my school. The stars are crossed no matter how I turn my head toward the future.

I walk back inside and find Weston.

Lure, belittle, keep my head on my shoulders and hold it high, condescend.

Do the right thing, for Luke.

He holds court with five or six kids: baseball, graduation, this or that teacher, and his new tattoo. The tat is fresh. He still has the bandage on his shoulder. He lets us peek at it—an engorged American flag flown from the sailor's fouled anchor encircled by a ship's steering wheel with *University of Kansas Navel R.O.T.C.* stenciled in black.

Weston shows how the tattoo sits high enough on his shoulder to be concealed by his regulation uniform. All by the book. The anchor has a fishing line caught around its base, and he can't explain why this tattoo is the symbol of true navy sailors. It just is. Don't ask. (Ms. Walters would love this: me thinking about symbols outside of English glass—and with a beer in my hand, no less. Maybe I should ask her about the fouled anchor in between her rapturous lectures about Hamlet and Walt Whitman. This could be my Walden Pond. I contemplate the fires of youth around a keg, and inside my head I wax poetic about the symbolic weight of Weston's tattoo. The fouled anchor points toward something beyond the literal here and now. It points to a meaning I can't quite grasp even though it pulls me down and entangles me in its fishing line. It does not point to beauty, or even something merely beautiful. It does not sing of truth. And it does not cause hope in my American soul. I want this night to be poetic. My desire for poetry eats itself alive. The poem will not be made of words, however. It will be a poem incarnate. I can feel this. But I don't know what it means.)

Weston wants a halo of barbed wire for the other arm.

I decide that the tattoo is hideous. And it is perfect too. It is perfect that he ran right out with his dad for his first tattoo as a sailor-to-be. Go, Principal Ames. Weston tells us that Ames has the same fouled anchor embedded in his flesh and on the same arm, but Weston added the flag despite the pain factor, "because you know what they say about 'No pain.'" There are high fives, and back slaps.

Conversation flows between topics, getting hot about Mrs. Wright's World History research paper, the Jayhawk navy battalion, or another pro player's RBIs. Liquid-electric jolts snap as I listen to the cacophony. I perch my hips on the couch's edge and take a fresh beer from an outstretched hand. I don't need the beer to fit in with the crowd or show off my ability to imbibe. I don't need the beer, but I want to be drunker. It is not so easy to get drunk unless you concentrate on keeping your glass refilled at all times. I take the liquid into my throat with the intent to make something happen. I have been a scared little girl. Now I will drink until I can be the person strong enough to forget who I am. I just need to get near enough to

Weston.

For Luke, for Lucy.

Music pounds. I sip. I move my hips with the beat. I am warm and ready.

All night I have given him my guaranteed-to-lure, widest doe eyes. I held an arm beneath my chest to prop it up just so. I stood tall and lean and arched my back. I wet my fingertips and smoothed the baby fine strands into the nape of my neck. I have tricked him up. This is the card I have waited years to play. I have been a "good enough" girl. I gave head, but I never gave out. This makes guys crazy for it. I am a trophy for guys like Weston. I know it. My head is thick with Luke and my mom and Mother Jones in a cauldron of lake water cooked by hot points of starlight.

Rebecca White, doomed to succeed.

I was born to flirt: Weston is sure he is the one hitting on me.

TRUTH IF YOU DARE

Flirt, lure, and then truth will set me free. That's the only plan.

My watch reads 12:07. I catch Tiff's eye as Weston pulls me into the spare room with the rumpled camping cots. I want Tiffany to see me go into the room with Weston. She raises an eyebrow at me and steps out of a tight circle of girls. I give her a quick smile and mouth to her I am okay. I shape the word "relax" with my lips.

I can't relax, of course. This is it. My plan: I will let him touch me and kiss me. For Luke. I set my jaw rigid with the anticipation of his narrow lips on my skin. He will think that we are going to go as far as he wants. I'll let him get hot and hard, and then I will tell him that I know what he did to Luke. I want to see his face when I say it. The thought of him tricked up by my willingness to seduce him and then rubbing Luke in his face, straightens my back. He will be afraid of me. I wave my shoulders, showing off my cleavage to Tiff, and she gives a laugh and waves me into the room.

(Enter R.)

214

His hand is tight and hot around mine. I force his fingers to interweave with mine. Laced fingers equals more than a casual flirtation; only a girlfriend holds her boy's hand with fingers twined. He thinks I am willing to do whatever he wants. He leans in and whispers, "Babe, you sure?" I say, "Let's go, let's go—everyone is staring at us," and we stumble into the room. As I pull the door behind me, I turn the lock. He smiles as I turn the metal bolt. I put his hand just above my waistband and he slips his fingers beneath my halter and starts.

We don't talk; a righteous speech writes itself in my head. I tell myself how easy he is making this for me. Poor Weston, it is almost like he wants to get caught in my trap. He must know deep down that it has come down to this: a girl who knows his game and can beat him at it with her eyes closed.

We move together onto the cot. I am hot between my legs, not warm or wet. Just hot. This is Weston after all— the kid who walks into a room and takes his pick of the girls. When he talks to a girl for the first time, she feels her life taking shape. Now I know how Luke must have felt when Weston held his arms while he drank from the funnel. The blond hair wants to be touched. His eyes are hard on the surface, yet when Weston focuses his baby blues on my face, I see glassy brilliance and I want to crack the icy blue and swim inside. Briefly, I want to hold him and tell him that his mother loved him and that his father is just a control-freak prick. Luke must have wanted to love him too. I understand him better now.

Weston slobbers on my neck and smothers my breast with his hand. The heel of his palm presses beneath my breast and then slips upward and grinds into the nipple.

Luke would never kiss a girl like this. My head fills with pinpricks of white starlight pain. Instead of a scream, I take small nips out of his shoulder, biting to hurt. He tenses, and then pulls back. "Weston, I am not sure I want to be your girlfriend." He says, "Why not, why not, we are so good right now." He takes pathetic bites out of my breasts. He thinks that I like the bites and he wants to get crazy with me. It hurts, and I feel like a porn star without the bright lights and cameras. What girl would want her tits incised and scathed by his vodka-soaked tongue?

The ceiling has spider-web cracks. Dust crusts the ceiling fan along the motor's casing. The bare light bulb has a chain reaching toward us, swaying. Or are we moving back and forth now?

I hate this room and plan to forget it as soon as I can. It is not too late to push him away from me and lure him back to the party. He will protest but play along—game for a tease if he thinks I would be a sure thing tomorrow or next week.

But then, what if I want him to touch me between my thighs? Maybe what Luke told me about that night here last fall (the hate, the blood) was not exactly the way it happened? Luke does not lie to me (what if he lies to himself?). Weston is kissing me and my body is hot and he bites to please me, even though it hurts me.

–Are you okay? He asks.

My legs are stiff as boards. The Spring Break party on the other side of the locked door is a lifetime behind me. The music has changed to a song with deep bass and pounds away, but I can't understand the lyrics. The noise vibrates across my sternum.

I am okay.

I look him in the eye and see my darling, Luke. He must have wanted Weston to make love to him too. Instead, Weston called Luke a cocksucker. And Luke believed him. Luke will never doubt Weston's judgment. We give him this power. All of us at school clear a path and pave it gold for him to walk between us like a god. He is beautiful on the outside and we want his perfect jawline, covered with stubble, to take us away from our ugliness. He is our movie star, our son of the principal, our hometown boy heading for the navy on a full ride NROTC scholarship to the school of his choice. He chose KU. He will reign in a fraternity. He will rule an ocean cruiser. Where will it stop? Who will bring him down?

Me. I am sure. I knew that Weston had to pay, and now that knowledge pushes out the pounding music and settles dead center in my chest. My ribs flare up as I suck oxygen deep into my lungs to feed the knowledge that blooms into certainty. Yes. Weston deserves to suffer the way Luke suffers, the way I have suffered for him. I let the certainty smolder inside of me, sure that it will blaze out and consume him.

The weight of justice nails me to the bed while my hands raise and circle his back. My arms wrap around blood, muscles, and bones. I press my palms flat against his broad shoulders. My skin is cold against his hot torso.

I will say it out loud, right out loud with no attempt to lower my voice or appear coy. I do not engage my famous doe eyes. I stare into the ceiling and steel myself against his reprisal: a punch, a knife, a hard dick.

Then it hits me: I'll let him think that I'm like all the other girls who love to blow him. I want him to call me a "cocksucker." Of course, he won't call me a cocksucker now when he is in the heat of it. Later when he knows he has been set up and taken down, he will. I slide out from beneath him. He rolls on his back like a good dog, ready to be stroked. My knees cram into the bare wood floor. He holds his dick in one hand and then it's in my mouth. I close my eyes. He is just another boy who thinks his dick tastes like candy. The gag rips at my throat as I force my jaw wide and restrain my teeth from clamping down. My hands curl on the rough blanket, my knuckles burn against the wool. He pushes my head down and down harder on his dick, but my head is just another part of my body. Rebecca is tucked away in my private memories of before Luke was invaded, before he told me about what Weston did to him, before I watched him fail out of high school and decide to love the drugstore girl. Rebecca, she waits until this business is done. She will emerge from this spare room the woman she was meant to be before she found herself on a dirty cot with a boy rapist who deserves to suffer.

I open my eyes with an inspired, improvised, new-and-improved plan of attack. I will scar him for life with a taint on his skin he can't wash off with the strongest of absolutions or hide beneath a navy uniform. I have the why, and now I have the how.

I can cry rape and he won't deny it if I threaten to tell the truth about Luke.

I tilt my head back and slither up to his face, my lips damp. He is a pig, an animal ready for slaughter. He is fattened up, and I will slit his gut and make sausage to feed the hungry and the weak. Kill the pig, roast his flesh. Kill the pig. I say, to his face,

–I know what you did to Luke.

His body stops while his mind tries to get it up against me.

–I'll tell everyone what you did. You piece of shit.

He is drunk, and his balls are blue, yet he knows this for what it is: hard-core, no turning back. It is what it is. And he knows he has already lost. This room is our crucible. Here we are. All these months he must have waited for Luke to trick him up. He didn't expect me, harmless good-girl Rebecca, to call him out. Set him up. Do him in.

He holds my arms down and looks me in the face. He calls Luke a "cocksucker" and me an "effing cunt." He laughs.

I call him a "rapist."

This is for real. No joke. He knows everything will come crashing down. He lurches toward the door and blocks it. He faces me, his eyes wild with fear. I scramble to my feet. I force my shoulders down and stick my chest out. I lunge around him for the door. I have to escape, otherwise who will believe me later when I tell them about Weston? How I tried to get away and how he forced me? He gets my ankle and latches his hand just above my sandal strap. He controls his voice, holding back hysteria, as he slams his fist into the floor and says "cunt" pulling me down and climbing on me. I do not fight him. I say, "no." Please, no.

I scrape my fingernails into the soft skin beneath his left eye. His dick is soft, an empty envelope of flesh.

He holds me down and I tell him again.

–I will tell everyone what you did to Luke.

Panic in his eyes: Fight or flight? I see his eyes seeing me for the first time as a girl with balls.

–The navy won't touch a shit like you. If you deny what happened tonight, I will tell everyone what you did to Luke.

His heart bursts from his chest. He has stopped listening to me; his eyes are closed. My threat festers on my lips. Then "rapist" fills my head and I scream.

–No!

After I say it the second time, it becomes a powerful chant.

–Shut up, you cunt.

–Let me go!

–Shut up or everyone will hear.

Exactly. The kids out there will hear. And kids tell. And then the lowest blow I can muster, delivered in a fierce whisper for his ears:

–You are so gay.

His fist unfurls toward my face. His knuckles come at me all tight and he is hitting my face—what if my nose breaks?—and pain blossoms in my neck, my lower back, my kidneys as I am kneaded by the force of his hand.

Then he is up pressing his meaty shoulder against the door. From the outside a key turns and the bolt slides. Someone is trying to get in the room, trying to decipher the screams. *My* screams.

My throat constricts and wild animal noises fill the room, seep into the cabin, and shake down the moon. The tide has changed, I think. My gut is the moon, exerting a gravitational pull and push on people near and far.

The room smells of dust, crawls with mites. Weston is gone. The pride dulls the pain in my face: I pulled Weston to me. I spoke the truth to this face, with his pants down. He wanted me, and he got me: now what will he do with me?

Luke is free now. *Then there's a pair of us — don't tell! They'd banish us, you know.* I didn't ask to be here, on my back, my blood wet metal on my tongue. I was chosen. I was told.

Tiffany is at my side. Mark carries me through the dead-silent house. The kids run. Car engines turn over, and tires crunch rocks as they grind down the dirt roads. Mark gets me into the backseat, and we are on the road. I am pain, and my lungs can't fill with air. The bone-deep ache takes me somewhere far away from the party, and I can see my long fingers, broken and bloodied, reach out to the blades of the ancient ceiling fan in the spare room where it happened. I won't forget that room, I realize, or the dust. When I try to open my eyes, the world spins beneath me and I do not cry. I glance at the dashboard and see the clock: 1:25. Mark drives with his hands firm around the wheel. Tiffany holds my head on her lap. She does not cry or ask me questions. She holds me and tells me that, It's going to be okay, you'll be fine. Repeat. She strokes my head and tells me that I am a brave girl and it is okay, will be okay. Everything will be okay. (Tiffany will be a good mom someday, her kids so lucky to have her. She doesn't tell me, Relax. I want to tell her, Relax, but I am beyond words, beyond the beyond.)

Mark and Tiffany fight about where to take me. They settle on her house because they need to think. The pain settles into a scream through my brain, but I can't hear it. I refuse to hear it.

PUBLIC

Like a frog. Tiffany croaks: Call the police.

Call (low, grating, bowel-wrenching, guttural yawp)

the (swallowed up in the dark of her parents' basement rec room)

police (sounds like puh-lease).

Her agonized pleas reach me when I turn my head toward her.

Call the police.

I sit straight and tall. I concentrate. My own eyelids press down. Blink. Blink. (Wink.) Blink.

Tiffany riffles through the Yellow Pages, sure there are hotlines for girls like me. I don't use the tissue Mark gives me to wipe tears or blood away from my face.

I sit. I hold the tissue in my fist.

She tells Mark to call the police. He waves his hands and says he is not sure what Rebecca wants.

It takes all my strength to sit.

Tiffany is loyal. This makes me cringe. How dreary. I am tired of myself after all.

She tears the phone away from Mark and says she will

call Luke.

    –My mom, call my mom.

    Tiffany dials by heart. The pallor on Mark's face must reflect my own.

UNIFORMS

Tiffany calls my mom and speaks in a hushed voice. She says I am okay but something happened and meet us at the hospital, okay?

Okay.

Uniforms appear next to the examining table at regular intervals. First the nurse: thighs swathed in stain-resistant polyester and all business. Height, weight, temperature, blood pressure. She quantifies me. This makes me calm. I am here. My height is the same. I have a normal temperature. My blood pressure didn't ring any alarms. I breathe in the sanitized air. The examining room is a perfect square. There is no ceiling fan.

Mom arrives at 4 a.m. and I marvel at how she roused herself from the sleeping pills. She must have stood outside my examination room and gathered her wits. Her eyes are two headlights turned bright, ready to see the danger even though it is well beyond the highway's edge. I bristle when she enters, a hard habit. She comes to me, and I lift my feet and recline on the table. She unfolds the thin plastic sheath and tucks me in, my hands outside the cover. She smooths my hair away from my forehead. She doesn't ask. She stands there and takes my hand. She doesn't tell me what to think, say, or feel. She holds my hand in both of hers. She believes me. She believes in me. Her presence allows me to gratefully close my eyes into a fitful sleep.

I wake now and then, and my mother always here. She holds my hand and keeps me whole even as my mind fragments on rewind-replay trips into the night. Her hands pull me toward morning. Toward dawn. She presses my hand between her palms in a silent prayer. She stands beside my bed even though I have said horrible things to her in the past that can't be taken back. Soon I will say things to the uniforms that can't be erased. I will tell them the facts, a story that can't be undone. To hold your daughter's hand despite all—that is a mother, I finally understand. I am grateful to see how simple it can be between us. How could I have wanted her to use words, when her hands are unfettered eloquence? No words at all, just hard, white, cold hands held—despite what can't be unsaid, what waits to be said.

For years I have wanted her to know me, to see me and tell me who I am. Now her hands tell me this: she is mother, I am daughter. Words would be wasted between us.

Words are necessary for the police uniforms that enter my room as I eat limp toast and sip juice. They want facts.

I give them my story.

It was a Spring Break party. (I don't mention Tiffany.) Lots of kids were there, maybe fifty? I know Weston from school. We went to a movie once with my friend and another guy. Everyone at the party was drinking. I don't really drink, but I had a beer. Then, you know, Weston, he flirted with me. We are both going to KU next year. We talked about college, dorm parties, and plans for the summer. He took me into the back room. We started to make out, mostly kissing. But I didn't want to go all the way with him, you know. He got real pissed when I pushed his hands away and told him I didn't want to be his girlfriend. He said fine, but undid his pants and asked me to blow him. I told him no. I said please, not tonight, not here. He scared me—his face changed and he looked at me like he didn't even know me. He was mad, hateful, and then he held my head down there and made me. It happened fast, and I couldn't believe it. He pumped my head. He said "cunt" and called me a "cocksucker." Said it was his party. Said, "Come on, be a good girl and do it." But he couldn't do it; his penis got soft. I tried to get up and run for the door, but he grabbed my ankle. (I lean down and point to the ugly red welts on my ankle for the uniform to note). He wanted to go all the way. (I wrap my arms tight across my chest and teeter on the exam table's hard edge.) He punched me in the face, and the next thing I knew my friend was driving me to her house. I didn't want to, but he made me. He made me do it; held my head and said he'd tell everyone I was just a "hard-core stone-cold bitch" if I didn't.

The police uniform takes detailed notes. The pen is loud against the notepad. (It is not a Bic). The uniform asks about my outfit last night. I say, *It's there on the chair*. The crumpled halter and jeans, abandoned on a chair, go into a plastic bag. What did I drink? One or two beers? Did I flirt with Weston first? Am I positive that I said "no"?

My mom holds my hand.

I tell the uniform, "Weston put his dick in my mouth—and he punched me and held me down." Those are the facts.

"Why would Weston attack you, Rebecca? Did you have an argument?"

I shrug my shoulders and say that I don't know why he did this. I always thought he was, like, an okay guy, you know?

The officer gathers the notes and the plastic bag with my ruined clothes, and leaves. I am free to go. I wasn't told that I was free to go. Part of me was afraid that somehow I would be charged with a crime or at least tricked up in the telling of the story. My heart rate, which was steady as steady goes, now starts to race. My heart can't escape my chest, but it wants to try. Weston grabbed my ankle and pushed me down. He punched me. These things happened, really, I tell myself.

The officers have my testimony and evidence too—my clothes and his skin scraped from beneath my fingernails. Soon a police photographer will document the slow-blooming bruises set to darken in the noon light.

I told a story: beginning, middle, and end. First, second, and then third and final act. But it is not my story. It is the facts. It is the truth. My heart throbs now with the fear that I will be found out by the cops. This must be the taint setting in: my skin bruised purple-black fading to orange and green, but my head bears the weight of what I have done. Luke will not be tainted. Instead my body, my life will bear it. I simply can't know that that will mean for me. I refuse to think about it. Yet I wouldn't change a thing, so far. It was the right thing to do, I tell myself. Words gather at the back of my throat and spill onto my lips. Words that could tell mom the truth—Weston raped Luke, I swear; not tonight, but last fall, and Luke told me, and I had to make Weston suffer—but she pats my hair and calls Dad. She asks him to bring my red sweats, a T-shirt, and my running shoes. She tells Dad to hurry; use the key under the back door. She hangs up and asks me if I want her to tell Dad what happened. She says I don't have to tell him. I can wait until things "settle down." I don't have to talk about it anymore, she promises, unless I want to talk about it, and then that is okay too. I hold her hand. She falls quiet with me. "Becca," she says, "you won't have to suffer anymore because of this." I decide to believe her.

A counselor arrives. (She is not wearing a uniform.) She brings coffee. She tells us in a matter-of-fact voice that she is here to help us in any way possible. My mom thanks her for her being there and clings to the cup. I take the coffee and drink the tepid brew, thick with sugar and creamer. I want to drink it hot, plain, and black, in the diner, with Tiffany and Luke.

Luke. Luke used to sit across from me in the diner with his white mug brimmed with coffee. He took the Bic pens tied up in ribbon for his birthday and wrapped his arms around me. He nuzzled my neck. He drove fast across the prairie at dusk. He trusted me to keep his secret. He fell in love with Jenni from KanMart.

I will call him soon, I think. I want to see him. I can't wait to see him now that Weston has paid. The thought of seeing him, of looking him in the eye, makes me feel like breathing again. Deep breaths of oxygen for brain, my heart.

The counselor sits on a metal folding chair pulled up to the foot of my bed. Her arms rest in her lap. She has done this before; she will do it again. Later she brings coffee one more time before we leave the hospital. She gives me her card—her name is Ms. Melissa Estes—and promises to call tomorrow. She must do this volunteer work for some reason, but I don't want to hear her story, not now or maybe ever. I told the facts to the cops, but I won't tell her my story. Not this morning. I am talked out. Besides, I can tell by the way she doesn't need or want to ask questions, she would see right through my story. There is a chance she would might still be on my side. Better to play it safe. Walk the walk. Alone.

THEN

I stay home from school. My mom takes Monday, Tuesday, and Wednesday off work. She hovers outside wherever I happen to be. She knocks on the bathroom door after five minutes to see if I need anything. She raps on the bedroom door at 11 am to see if I want to wake up. How about a glass of pineapple juice? Some cinnamon-sugar toast? Her voice is soft, pleading. Kind.

Dad stays with us. He sleeps on the living room couch and uses his own tube of toothpaste. Now and then I walk in on my parental exes: voices hushed, my mother uncrossing her arms when she notices me in the doorway.

Dad sits and watches daytime television with me—morning news programs with cheery banter, soap operas filled with passionate looks, game shows with has-been celebs—until it occurs to him midweek to rent a bajillion movies.

By Thursday late afternoon we are one with the couch, our pajamas in need of rotation. We start to disagree over movie titles and then over the remote control. We are tired of sugary cereal for dinner. Mom tried to make us healthy and hot meals, but I refused her efforts to restore my health. Dad has eaten bowl after bowl of artificially colored cold cereal in a show of solidarity. It's sweet.

By Friday I find myself waiting for the Oprah show. My fascination with Oprah is real. I gush hot tears as her guest confesses her addiction to shoplifting. Today the show will be about "women who love too much." It occurs to me that I could write to Oprah a letter detailing my story (or Luke's story). I compose drafts in wild daydreams between naps in the afternoon sunlight. Surely, to write Oprah would tempt the gods-on-high to strike me down. What if I had written to Oprah months ago and given her Luke's story? Someone in a tailored suit and good shoes would have swooped into town and flown me first class to their studio. The hot camera lights, the touch of makeup to fight my shiny skin, and then the leading questions. Tears would have been involved. Lots of tears.

Others, just like Luke and me, could be warned or even saved. I was motivated to save other potential victims. But, deep down, right now, I don't care if any others exist. They don't exist. At least, not like Luke and me. Not really. Our story is our story. I stepped up and did my dance for Weston and the uniforms. I did what I could. I am just Rebecca, after all—a girl in Kansas, where the wind parches the land. Oprah doesn't deserve our story.

Mom arranged for me to see a therapist on Saturday. She drove me to the appointment and waited in the parked car. The therapist's office looked like a cozy living room on the set of a New York sitcom. I sank into the soft leather couch and threw the blanket she offered over my shoulders to fight the chill in the air-conditioned room. She smiled a forehead-crunched smile, and I got that she was serious, concerned, and very professional. She had a short brown bob and was dressed in soft earth tones. Her shawl trailed in a ribbon of deep cranberry toward white carpet. I took a hard, long look at the plush white carpet and sank into the cold leather couch with a sigh. One hour seemed an eternity. My journalism skills kicked in, gave me a reason to look her in the eye, and I asked her my questions:

How does this work?

Can she tell anyone what I say?

Will she keep a record of what I say?

It turns out that she has to report to the authorities if I threaten to hurt myself or someone else. The good part about that, I think, is that the hurt has already been done.

I give the therapist credit: She listens very well. Even for the long minutes I sit there with my eyes glued to the singular speck of dirt to mar the carpet. Before I know what is happening, sentences erupt from my throat despite my fear of soiling the pretty neutral walls with my ugly self. I don't talk about Weston, not yet. I "need time." I am willing to take my time.

I talk about school—my fear of going back to face all that. I describe the uniforms and how, after I told them about that night, I felt dirty and clean at the same time. The telling of it, when I finished and the cop had gone, left me dizzy and light and, well, free. I thought I was going to be in trouble. I can't shake the feeling that it was my fault somehow. I talk about Dad staying with us, the movies, and the cold cereal. I talk about Oprah and how I want to be a guest on her show—battered, formerly fat, eternally sad—yet triumphantly clinging to a sliver of hope in the goodness of strangers. (I want to believe that strangers will buy the story; my word, Rebecca's word, against his.)

I don't talk about Luke. Or Weston. What point would there be in telling Luke's story now? It is finished. The tragedy undone. A new chapter has begun for him, even if he may not know it yet.

When she asks me if I want to see her again, I say, okay. But I never go back.

LUCY

Weston is in juvenile lock up. He made threats against me in front of the officers when they took him in. So they can hold him until the trial starts. But there might not be a trial if he pleads guilty. I am convinced that he will plead guilty. He must.

I told the police about Lucy. I didn't tell the police about her long, lean legs wrapped around Weston on that blanket or how she drank cheap beers to fight that night's summer heat. She dated Weston and then disappeared. They found her in Kansas City with her family.

Lucy told the police that Weston had gotten all control-freak on her. Suggested—by saying her new jeans made her look fat, that her favorite summer halter made her look like a slut—she wear certain clothes. Convinced her to give him the answers in calculus. She started to lose weight; then she lost all her friends. When she tried to break it off, he called her, crying. She raced over to his house, and he collapsed in her arms and told her that if she broke up with him he would kill himself. He had a gun. He didn't have it with him, but she had seen it before. He was so weak, he said. Could she forgive him? She did.

When she got pregnant, he drove her to the next town for an abortion.

When she broke down the next day and told her parents, the screaming match fizzled into funeral sobs while Lucy told them about Weston. She told them how she loved him still, Weston. First they confronted Weston and his dad. Principal Ames regretted Lucy's "situation" and said he was sorry for Lucy and her family, who were devastated by their little girl lost. But nothing illegal happened, he said with a shake of his head. He told Lucy's parents that it was done, best to move on. They did. The family packed up their bags and got out of town with their girl, what was left of her body and spirit.

Her parents drove Lucy back to town a few days ago. She gave her statement to the prosecutor about Weston.

I wonder who she loves now. I don't see her while she is in town. I suppose if I had asked, my mom could have arranged it. The thought of meeting Lucy makes my stomach tighten. I don't want to see what she has become. Maybe things are better for Lucy now, I hope. But if things are bad—she has gained 200 pounds or wears a turtleneck and long sleeves to hide her self-soothing razor cuts—I don't want to see it. I don't want to talk about Weston with her. Yet I don't know how to make small talk with her. Right. There are some things that even I am not capable of faking. I hope she has moved on.

Move on, Lucy, keep moving.

PROM

One week after the party, and it is prom night. One never-ending week. I stay home and wear pajamas, adding a touch of pearl-pink lip gloss to honor the occasion. Luke is taking Jenni to the prom, I guess. He wouldn't have gone with anyone else. He didn't ask me. I would have said yes. I would have said, Yes. My whole body wants to say yes to Luke. I wish it were that simple. It used to be that simple.

Tiffany and Mark stop by the house. Tiffany's yellow gown melts around her. She looks pretty. Mark looks like a little boy whose mother combed his hair for the first day of school. He opens the car door for Tiff, carries her purse while she adjusts her shoulder straps, and rat-a-tap-taps his fingertips on the kitchen table. We sit around the table for a few long minutes guessing at words that might fit the space left to us after Tiff's dress was carefully seated, her ankles crossed. The kitchen air is thick with perfume and aftershave.

Mark's fingers tap out his private trying-to-be useful tune on the kitchen table, and Tiffany's forehead contracts into furrows of pain on my behalf. I have to miss prom, she must be fretting, compounding my tragedy into something epic.

I give us all a break and show them her my scholarship letter from KU. Turns out I did earn a full ride: books, tuition, and room and board. The letter arrived that morning. I asked my dad to open it. When his eyes lit up all Fourth of July, I knew. So, no prom, but happy prospects for next year. A cosmic scale balanced, perhaps, it may seem.

Tiffany got a letter too, she gushes as she smooths her yellow gown from her thighs to her knees. She says she got a scholarship (she doesn't say full ride) to KU and a President's Scholarship to Newman College. She doesn't say she has decided to go to Newman, but the way she mentions it after KU, and leans her head toward Mark in acknowledgement of some private decision they have already sealed, I know.

I take out my camera, a pretty decent Canon my mom got me secondhand after I proved what I could do with the school's camera. They pose by the fireplace, with his arm around her shoulder, her hand clutching a tiny yellow purse. Dressed to kill and heading up the court in a fast break toward a two-point basket to beat the graduation buzzer. Their muscles flexed beneath skin taunt with the indescribable promise of prom night. They have earned this night of glamour and gloss. They are determined to have a good time regardless of any obstacles; they are determined to have fond memories.

Two photogenic smiles beam at me despite my greasy hair and days-old sour pajamas. I vow to give them copies and shove them out the door with good-natured concern that they will be late for their dinner reservations at the new steak house. It is a real restaurant with place settings and tablecloths. Tiffany must be ecstatic. She glows. I imagine her reading the menu with her spine pressed into the cold pleather booth. No, she would never choose a booth. She will request a table to show off her dress. She will sit with her legs crossed while she chooses her main dish, careful to choose a mid-priced steak. She will nibble. Later she will cling to Mark on the dance floor, grateful to be Tiffany (and not Rebecca). Grateful to have Mark (and not Weston). Grateful. To have it all.

Tiffany hugs me again, and I touch the hairs at the base of her updo. She does look like a princess. I whisper in her ear to check her teeth for food or pepper shards before they pose for prom pictures. She smiles at me, her eyes bright and alert.

I shut the door and run to the living room couch. Kneeling on the couch, I watch them through the curtains. Mark opens the car door for her. Before he drives off toward the night of their lives, he gets the perfect on-the-road-with-my-prom-date music cued. They turn the street corner and I turn to sit and face the blank television screen.

My cold feet need to find a cozy pair of socks. My dad is getting more movies and pizza. Mom is across the street at a neighbor's house, chatting about the lawn or who knows what. The house is mine for a few moments, and I settle into the fridge's hum, the odd moan from beneath the carpet or gurgle-chuck from the icemaker. This is my house. I have a scholarship. I will graduate.

I haven't spoken to Luke since before the Spring Break party. Before.

Luke didn't witness the incident at the party, but I am

sure Tiffany (and legions of others) reported every shred of information. He must know the story: how Weston forced me, and how he is in custody now. But Luke hasn't called me. I haven't called him. The phone sits on the coffee table next to the couch. It is alive and magnetic. It urges my fingers to dial. It is easy to punch in his numbers, put the phone to my ear. Speak.

I take the phone into my hands. I touch the numbers— press my fingertips without punching the soft plastic discs. The longer I keep my vigil by the phone, the less likely it seems he will ever call me again.

I could dial the phone; I want him to call me first.

I relinquish the phone into a sea of movies and a few half-filled glasses of Coke diluted with melted ice. I lay my head down on the armrest and push my soft stomach out as far as it will pouch beneath my elastic waistband. The air is stale inside the house; I smell. It is about time for a hot shower and a hair wash. My fingernails are atrocious— chipped and torn (and chewed). My face is bloated. I pick at my heel callous and feel the need to pumice and polish. It is time for me to get out of the house.

Luke will not call. That night in Weston's lake house, beneath the ceiling fan, I thought I had a stroke of genius. In an instant, I thought I had the entire scenario figured out. Yet I hadn't foreseen what Luke would see. I was so busy trying to make it right for Luke that I never stopped to think what it had to look like from his perspective. The days on the couch provided enough commercial time for my brain to meander into Luke's head and see me and the incident the way Luke must understand the events of that night. There is one conclusion: he has ample motive to despise me now. I pick up the phone and set it on my belly.

It sits there, benign and inert. How could he call after what I have done? After what he thinks I must have done?

It looks bad from Luke's perspective: I hooked up with Weston. The halter top. Tiffany saw me wink-and-smile as I followed Weston in the back room. My boobs. Others must have seen my little show and been convinced too. Luke thinks I am the queen of all that is vile and wrong with this world. I can't tell him that it was a trap. If I tell Luke that I set the whole thing up, then the secret will be loose in this world. And secrets do their work in this town. I don't trust the world. I trust myself.

I keep secrets. Luke told Ms. Turner the school counselor about his fear that he is gay—this is just one more piece of evidence that he is a talker. He is a talker. I have adored him for years because he finds all the right words to fix any awkward moment. He used to make me shine even when I knew deep down that I did not deserve his attentions (and even deeper down, I knew that he made everyone feel like they were worthy of attention, praise, and friendship). The price I have to pay to keep my word, prove my friendship, and prove my worth is off any scale and more and more steep. I promised Luke I would protect his secret, and now I have to protect his innocence, keep him ignorant of what I have done in his name. This I believe: Luke deserves to be clean. To have a chance to be Luke.

Losing Luke is a price that had not occurred to me until it had already happened. It has happened, I tell myself, and I have myself to blame. I can't tell Luke that I trapped Weston; now I may have lost Luke forever. Luke thinks I betrayed him. And I can't set him straight.

I didn't lose Luke to Jenni. I lost Luke thanks to my own

need to set him free. He is free now. Free from Weston. Free from me.

I could call him, but what could I say to make this go away? To make it all better, there there. As if I could nonchalantly invite him for a slice of peanut butter pie at the diner? Hardly.

BACK TO SCHOOL

The seniors simmer with post prom analysis, finals, and looming graduation events. A constant, low emotional heat keeps us all popping toward graduation. Weston is still in Juvenile Detention. Principal Ames took a leave of absence for the remainder of the year.

Tiffany drives me to school, meets me for lunch at our usual table, and takes me home. But she can't be with me all the time. Gossip prickles my skin during Ms. Walters's English class and settles into a knot at the base of my neck in the dark whir of the overhead projector during World History. At the end of the day, I give the following grades:

Teachers get an A for being discreet. They pretended business-as-usual and recommended appointments after school to conference about late assignments.

Kids get a C because they are juvenile—gossip, anxiety, and drama as expected. (But I detest them for it anyway.)

Tiffany gets an A+ for support.

Luke gets a C for not being in school—as expected.

Rebecca gets a D for being terrified the whole day that someone would confront her and pissed that no one did.

D equals less than satisfactory in all aspects. I do not get an F because I have never gotten an F and can't sink that low no matter what happens.

TIFFANY UPDATE

The second day back to school I inhale and exhale often enough to control a massive, blistering headache behind my doe eyes.

After school Tiffany drives us to her house to get some textbooks and a pot of turkey chili her mom wanted to send over to us.

We drop the stuff in the kitchen and head to my bedroom. Keeping my back to Tiffany, I unbutton my shirt and let it crumple on the mess of rejected clothes next to my unmade bed. Pick up a soft, oversized T-shirt.

This morning I redressed at least six times (and a half) and left the rejects where they fell in my determination to find the right look. I wanted to look: decent, a good kid, unremarkable. It was important to wear plain, unexcitable colors and blend into the hallway crowds as much as possible. I settled on a navy button-down shirt with white piping along the collar and my baggy jeans. I can't believe how much I cared about creating my fashion façade. It was agony to decide. It was easier than letting myself contemplate the day ahead, sure to be filed with stares or pointed non-stares, not to mention the stacks of make-up papers and missed tests.

Tiffany picks up a few pairs of discarded jeans and folds them over my desk chair. She makes half-hearted, feeble attempts to untangle the rat's nest. Then she excuses herself to get Cokes from the fridge. We need sugar and caffeine, she says.

My head is thick with sleep, and I want to curl under my comforter and sleep away all my head tripping. Instead I find my sweatpants, and the soft material cocoons me.

When I follow Tiff to the kitchen, she has two glasses of ice ready and waiting for Cokes. She drags the soup pot onto the back burner and gently reports the gossip from school as she stirs.

Truth: It turns out that the school had decided my fate mere days after the attack, before I even showed my face.

I flirted with him. Everyone says that I have been obsessed with him all year long. True. In the crowded cafeteria, I always managed to find an open table near him. I gave him big lovey-dovey eyes. I invited him to a movie and then took him out for dinner. I have been after him, and maybe I've even crushed on him for years, they say. I wore that skimpy top to the party. Besides: everyone knows that Rebecca is a tease—pretty girl who doesn't go quite all the way. So why should they feel sorry for me if I asked for it?

They are sorry about the scandal; but, really, they are happier it didn't happen to them—especially the guys.

It hurts. My brain freezes everything Tiffany reports into tiny little snowflakes, heaps up the snow banks, the edges stained with dog urine and black road sludge. My head is a blizzard, emotions frozen into stabbing icicles.

I should be hot with anger. Instead I feel hollow.

Those kids at school haven't seen the true colors of my bruises. Weston didn't do me the favor of a public injury, no broken nose or fractured ankle requiring a heavy white cast. They didn't see the scarlet bruise he smeared across my face. Before I went back to school yesterday, I spent long minutes in front of the bathroom mirror covering the mess with a thick icing of flesh-colored foundation. A light sprinkling of face powder concealed the bruise, even though I thought it made me look like a walking corpse. My ankle is still swollen and bruised from his desperate grab to hold me down. The nurse iced it at the hospital. The kids at school can't see the physical evidence against Weston. The ones at the party, even. They were there at the party; they saw us explode from the room. But they can't see it anymore, have considered the circumstances and decided the facts, as they see them, are enough to convict me. Instead of Weston.

All day I took small, measured steps because of my ankle. I didn't want to flinch in pain. I didn't wear a short skirt, the kind that used to make me swagger down the hall like a girl going places (other than English class). I wore my old jeans and a plain shirt like a regular kid. I kept to myself. But the kids won't allow that. They feed off the drama. Rebecca versus Weston. The game of the century.

Tiffany tells me ever-so-gently between long drinks of Coke the whole deal as she can gather it, because, of course, she is not too popular either being the friend of Rebecca White.

Yes, they think Weston is rough around the edges, even a violent kid. He shouldn't have hit me. Maybe his dad is violent, they speculate, even though no one has evidence to support the theory. Yes, they think that I am a tease. I didn't deserve to be attacked, but he didn't deserve to be accused either. He didn't rape me, after all; it was just a blowjob. They don't think it is fair that I screw up his life forever. I can get over the trauma of Weston getting rough with me. But Weston lost his NROTC scholarship to KU. The navy will not take him now (or ever) with a sexual-assault charge on his record. His life is ruined, they say. His dream deferred. His future derailed because of one night's out-of-control party and one girl who drank too much and teased him and then got all weepy about the consequences. Besides, they say, he is just the kind of guy who would thrive in the navy. He is rough around the edges, true; military discipline would have worn him down into a fine man. Just like his dad. Now he is stripped of his chances to make something of himself; he is ruined. Because of Rebecca White, you know, *that* girl. Really, it is such a shame. It was only a blowjob, after all. And Principal Ames is wrecked—his neighbors saw him out last week after midnight. He was unshaven and jogging. He ran himself ragged for at least three hours, making wide loops around the subdivisions. The sweat streamed down his face; some said it wasn't perspiration, but his own tears. (Please.)

It's creepy that Ames jogged by my house.

Tiffany reaches across the table and touches my arm, her hand interrupting her monologue, to reassure me that she merely reports these things. She is angry and indignant on my behalf. (Without Tiff, where would I be?)

She stirs the chili con carne. The thick soup bubbles and pops. The topic changes from the muddled to the mundane. She describes for me all the brochure details about Newman College—the different dorm room options and the classes she hopes to enroll in during Freshman on Campus Day this summer. Tiffany says I should apply next year. She thinks that maybe I should, like, take the year off and travel or whatever before I start college. She can get a single room this year and wait until her sophomore year to get a double with me. She is so kind to me. I wish I were able to ask her put the spoon down. Sit. Listen. I want to tell her the whole story. But I can't do that to her. I can't give her the burden. The truth is sometimes too much. She is my only friend now. I will spare her. If I tell her, it will ruin her life. It is asking too much. I want her to go to college. I want her to be free—really free.

Anyway, Tiffany has romantic notions about taking the year off. In her family, this might mean a year in Spain immersed in language study where the locals teach you all the bad words and stuff you with fresh bread, cheese, and olives. Or it could mean a character-building year on a reservation in Arizona teaching dark-skinned children to read and solve story problems.

For me, Rebecca White, a year off from college would mean working at the movie theater or the mall, making a few extra bucks, and living full time with my mom. The house shrinks each day. We entered a silent pact to settle down into our quiet life. But. My brain grows numb between inane sitcoms and sensible dinners of chicken and broccoli.

I will eat chili for dinner with my mom. I will simmer through the next few weeks, graduate, and move on. Somehow. Somewhere.

Tiffany takes off around six to head home. On her way

out, she oh-so-casually mentions her graduation party and asks if I am still planning one with Luke. Honestly, I had managed to forget the whole deal. Luke's ambition for a grand graduation gesture. The graduation party: one more torture to endure. I will have to call Luke about the party. After all, it was his last wish before Weston got him, before I got Weston.

Tomorrow. I'll call Luke tomorrow, I tell myself.

True or False:

_____ 1. Rebecca will call Luke tomorrow.

_____ 2. Tiffany is a loyal friend.

_____ 3. Rebecca deliberates about her clothing—"baggy jeans and navy button down shirt with white piping along the collar"—for her return to school. She wants to become invisible.

_____4. Rebecca has committed a crime.

_____5. Rebecca is guilty.

_____6. If you were Rebecca, you would have done the same thing.

_____7. Rebecca doesn't deserve Tiffany as a friend.

_____8. If you were Luke, you would *never* call Rebecca after what she has done.

_____9. There is no truth.

_____10. Rebecca will crack and tell *someone* the truth(s).

CHAPTER SIX

THE FINAL EXAM

Luke's mom calls two weeks before graduation about party plans. She tells me how sorry she is for my troubles and how she thinks I am a brave girl doing the right thing. I say, Thank you. She has perfected her recipes, and she thinks we should arrange the decorations—balloons, streamers, and maybe some sparklers too? I don't have the heart to cancel the party.

Luke and I talked face to face.

After a full week back to school, he called on Friday afternoon. We agreed to meet.

On Saturday morning he comes over to the house. We sit on my back porch. He notices the scorch marks. So I tell him how I made a little bonfire of my vanities the night before I left for Christmas break (76 days after Luke told me). I admit I burned every single binder and spiral—sparing anything before high school. The middle school reports and kindergarten art projects were preserved because they seemed too innocent to suffer the flames. First I burned my school notebooks. I burned all the notes that Luke had ever written to me. When he hears my confession, he throws his hands up in the air, rising up to his full height as if to go to my room, find the notes and prove my bluff. I am not lying, and it's much too late by now, of course, to save them or take back my burnt offerings.

I tell him that I burned the whole mess of spirals and notes out of deep frustration. I felt so—helpless—and the idea of putting flame to my notes had been so simple and compelling. I told him it was like someone else found the matches and cleared the patio. The flames had been quick and fair in their devastation. It was beautiful.

I don't tell him that the long weepy notes and the silly gossip incriminated him—made him the same as any other stupid high school kid. A few of his notes had seemed poetic when I first read them back in ninth grade. As I read them before I consigned them to the flames, however, they were ridiculous and painfully cute. I am sure my notes to him are filled with the same romantic visions of friendship and love. To make things even, it occurs to me that he should purge our history with a bonfire of his own, my notes the kindling for the flames. I don't ask him to burn my notes. The air is already acrid enough.

I don't tell him what I burned afterward, the thick stack of pages with images and details from my research about what happens to boys who are raped. How it happens. How it can never be undone. How the victim is tainted. How the truth told does more harm than good: the boy becomes a fag. I burned all those research pages on the ashes of his notes and my classwork.

We sit. I pull my knees up to my chest and sink deep into the dusty plastic chaise lounge. He sits with his broad shoulders arched back into a bow, his elbows on his knees, his face a tight fist.

–Tell me everything that happened. I want to hear it from you.

I give him credit for wanting to hear my side of the story.

–Tiffany and I went together, but Mark came later, and then I was on my own. I didn't plan to seduce Weston and get locked in the spare room. Everything happened fast, and I fought him, I swear. Tiffany and Mark drove me to the hospital, and my mom came. She was there and held my hand while the police asked me questions. The nurse did an exam. She put stuff up inside of me, probing and scraping. The room, at the lake house, had this ceiling fan, and it was coated layers of dust ten years deep. I wanted to talk to Weston, Luke, but I didn't know what to say. So I waited—this whole time—and watched until I could get near him. How can I say this? I wanted to get close to him and make him see me, really know me, and then I thought I could, you know, get him to see that you are my friend and what he did was wrong. And I wanted him to be sorry. But I didn't know how to put any of that into words. So I followed him into the room with the cot. I thought I was stronger than him. Not that I was physically stronger, but I was right and he was wrong and I thought that mattered. I thought being right would somehow make things turn out right.

(I lean forward and mirror Luke's posture: knees planted apart, elbows on knees. I soften my face into an open plain where the fierce wind blows down trees. I turn my palms up and then fold them pressed toward his heart):

–Tiffany heard me scream, Luke.

Then Luke asks me *the* question, "How could you have done this to me?"

What can I say?

Luke has every right to build a wall with accusations and hate. I stirred the wet cement with silence for weeks. Luke's exquisite anger and his deliberate speech, his heavy words and his question—the question—concrete my fate. I am walled in, still alive, bonded to Luke's image of me. It is an image that can't be consigned to a bonfire on the patio. An image beyond my powers to erase. I am a negative of myself, framed by Luke's vision of me. He traps me beneath his outraged sense of betrayal. Yet he leaves a hole for the oxygen to reach my tired lungs and for my eyes to see his face. His angry face backlit by the betrayal I had engineered to save him. Irony's iron bars on my prison cell.

Luke says,

–The least you could have done was to tell me the truth: you liked Weston all along. Do not protest. Let me talk. You like him more than you valued our friendship, obviously. I told you everything. And you told me nothing. You said "Weston is a rapist" and what he did to me was "wrong." But you were all talk. You obviously didn't mean any of it. You went to the lake house because you couldn't resist being with him—being at his lake party. Tiffany told me that you smiled at her as you went into the room with him. How could you flirt with him? Repulsive. You are horrible, Rebecca. You are sick. You think the rules don't apply to you—that you can have whatever you want, no matter who you have to hurt. You thought I'd forgive you or something once you could prove that he is some nice guy or something. I don't know who you are anymore, but you are not my friend. You are a stranger to me. Whatever you meant to accomplish in that room, I'm sorry that you got hurt, but you put yourself in that room. You always think that you can get away with controlling people who are less than perfect—like me, like Tiffany, and you thought that you could get Weston too—claim him as a prize or something, to prove that you are Rebecca White, the queen bitch of us all.

Queen bitch, his words, at last. He keeps talking after that, but I can't listen as his accusations play a scornful fugue inside my skull. I am a stranger to Luke, he said, in his own words. All along he resented that I was a "queen bitch," and now he has the evidence to convict me. He used to praise me, high-five me, and write me long congratulatory notes when I got the best of some jerky ex-boyfriend. When I confronted Lisa Monroe in eleventh grade, telling her that I knew she had spread rumors about me because she was jealous of my boyfriend, Luke was the first person to call me after school and report that Lisa was shamefaced. We ate pie at the diner after I told off Lisa, and he ordered my favorite, banana cream, to split between us.

Tonight on the patio with Luke I become a stranger to myself too. My dry eyes hurt. Metal pliers clamp on my temples, press and turn my scalp until an old-lady face stares into every reflective surface, my little-girl eyes scared beneath the sagging lids and canyoned ridges in my forehead. I tug at my T-shirt neckline and shift my weight from side to side in a self-soothing rock-a-bye. Better to be a stranger to Luke than tell him the truth of what I have done. My bones grow cold with loneliness as I allow Luke's rejection deep inside my marrow. The best thing to do from here until forever: lock up the story of what happened to Luke somewhere where it can't be retold. I'll talk about what Weston did to me, my attack over and over, until the telling becomes second nature. This is my last, great high school final exam. I will never move on from Luke. But if I can pass this last test, I can move out of this town. And never look back. Banished for my crimes.

Exiled. Sentenced to live in a world with Luke near enough to run into at the grocery store, shopping for milk and eggs, but never to share a pot of coffee or a slice of pie at the diner. Never to share the nearness of him, the intimate friendship that is content to be together without knowing too much. From the moment that night in his car, the night bright without stars, when he confided in me, I have known too much and he can't bear it. That alone would have been enough to end our friendship. But now he doesn't know enough about what I have done, and he can't bear that either. I was his launching pad, and now I am a tether, a chain, a necessary target.

Luke left the house after 45 minutes. He was on his way to see Jenni. I let him go. It hurt me to let him go—to her, especially. I walked him to his car and watched him drive away, and when I turned back toward my house I shook with sobs. I didn't attempt to plead my case with him while I had him face-to-face. After all, I did ask to use the funnel, and I did flirt with Weston—and Luke needed to know both of those things. He needs to believe that my betrayal is his greatest wound. He will remember me with disgust. The wound I induced will burn deeper and fester longer, cancelling the pain inflicted by Weston months before. He will forget Weston and instead condemn me. In this way I have freed him from Weston. Luke will not be tainted.

This is how it must be. I will be the real Nobody (*who are you?*), without my Luke. There used to be a pair of us nobodies. But I am banished into being the worst kind of Nobody—I am a Somebody because I am now the girl who accused Weston, ruined his naval career.

Hi, I am Rebecca White, I'll say.

And they will think, Oh yeah, Rebecca White, *that* girl.

Luke has Jenni from KanMart to kiss his cheek and turn him into her darling Luke after all. I am happy for him—or at least I will try to learn how to be happy for him. I will try. No one will know his name. He will never have to be *that* Luke.

REHEARSAL

We march two-by-two, mostly. I, Rebecca White, line up next to Cynthia Weixelman, and McKenzie Zimmer follows us to bring up the alphabetical rear of the class. We are used to being at the end of the line after all these years. Cynthia smiles at me and McKenzie manages to make small talk about KU. We have known since freshman year that we would walk the walk together. We struggled to construct a friendship on our alphabetical allegiance in the frantic first weeks of ninth grade before we settled into being polite locker buddies. They are in marching band, but I quit clarinet after sixth grade. I can barely tune the radio dial much less sing or read a note of music. Forget about moving my feet and playing an instrument.

Now the two of them, a clear pair, are miffed to march next to me in the cloud of ill-at-ease that surrounds me. They want to celebrate, not take a position on my moral standing. They march toward college sororities, successful careers, and boyfriends who will make great fathers, while I am still running away from my new reputation. I should invest in some good shoes—maybe a sensible pair of hiking boots for all terrains.

We practice the slow-step procession twice. Then we go through the motions of the entire ceremony, including the valedictorian and salutatorian speeches. I climb the rickety stairs to the platform and test *one-two-three* into the microphone. Two days ago I was told that a committee of teachers and staff had considered cumulative grades up until spring semester and I was ranked second to Geoffrey Hickle. It was no surprise. Geoff was always a step ahead of me; his persistent pattern of perfect papers irked all of us. (*Let's look at this student model to learn how to compose an effective essay.* The name crossed out, but his ideas effortless on the page.)

I don't have to recite my speech today, thankfully since I have not yet written a single word. I stand up tall on the stage with blank pages and practice modulating my volume: Testing, testing, one-two-three.

Luke doesn't come to rehearsal. When the vice principal called his name, he isn't here to take his practice walk across the stage. His alphabetical bookends were told to keep him in line on the big day. They will oblige (if he comes).

Luke has a habit of being more here (to me) when he is not here. He must be with Jenni, I think.

CHARGES

Juvenile Court is not held in the ornate stone courthouse in the heart of downtown. The regular courthouse is dignified. Portraits of old judges and town founders line the dark-lit corridors. Dust covers the windowpanes like permanent unlovely frost, the opaque panes too high for more than annual dusting, I imagine. Filtered light disperses long minutes, and hours spiral into a chamber of daydreams. High school kids on tours for government class lower their voices and step lightly. Juvenile court, on the other hand, is all fluorescent, all the time. No exterior windows. Grey paint coats the hallways. Even the defiant click of expensive heels is reduced to a cheap thwack.

Principal Ames called my mom, who called our lawyer, who called the prosecutor. The prosecutor called Ames's lawyer, and now the team of lawyers is waiting for my mom to join them. I didn't have to come to Juvenile Hall for the meeting, yet I couldn't sit at home either. Here I am.

The prosecutor, Mrs. Cruz, will press charges—the

exact nature and number of charges take quite a bit of conversation to nail down. It's so complicated, technical. She told me I didn't have to be a part of the process, that she could press charges on my behalf. I told her that I am willing and able to do what it takes to put Weston in jail. She told me how brave I am and then pulled me to her.

She said, "Honey, don't pin your hopes and your healing on his going to jail. We have a strong case with the bruises. We can prove that he beat you up. But Lucy's story is hearsay evidence. It bears no relevance in your case and can't be used in court. (Rumors can destroy you with their brutal force. Yet rumor has no strength, no cutting edge in the court of law.) And no one else was in the room. The kids breaking in the door to answer your screams prove that you were in distress—not necessarily sexual in nature. I promise you that Weston will be punished for assault, resisting arrest, and a bevy of other minor charges."

Despite these assurances, the black-and-white consensus holds: Weston Ames does not deserve to lose his navel career (subtext: can we lose another American soldier?) because of a high school party gone bad (subtext: It was just a blowjob.)

Principal Ames said the same to my mother on the phone. "Let's be real, here. It was just a blowjob and both kids had experience with that." He implied, of course, that it was not my first time.

Mom sat me down right there and then, asked me to tell her everything she might need her to know to help make a case against Weston. For me, the bruises spoke my most eloquent defense, not to mention the screams, and the kids who had to bust the lock and pull me away from him. But the blowjob is the heart of the matter. It throbs in the imagination. People just can't seem to wrap their minds around it. It was, after all, just a blowjob. Get over it, the accusatory faces at school say every time I stumble into eye contact. I had done that before but everyone knew that I hadn't had sex—that I wouldn't have sex with anyone until I was married. Former steady boyfriends of mine could testify to my failure to give it up.

More than sex, I have always wanted to drink strong, dark coffee and make talk with deep-down friends. Friends, like Luke, who know that we could shine light on the world's injustice (in short, make a difference). I wanted to drive my own rugged green jeep. My bones ache for the wind in my hair, the road flattening toward the horizon, taking me to a job where my hands would build something of use in this world. Business meetings. Coffee breaks. Budget problems. Mergers. Non-profits. Stocks. 401ks. True, my grasp of what these things mean is hazy at best, but when I think about "traveling for business" my shoulders square and my heart races. Tiny toothpaste tubes and sanitizing hand wipes seduce me. I want to walk with a purpose through an airport with no time to stop and adjust my picture-perfect lipstick.

I wanted life to be more than this awful, wet bog of guilt and confusion. I am tired of being alone in this game. I want dry land. I don't want to be reduced to desires that end in pain. Sex gets in the way. I didn't want to play that game. Or let it play me.

I can't wait until I have my own bills—house payment, electric, and water—to pay using a thick stack of checks signed using a thick slash of black ink. Yes, I will get a cat and call her Ms. Clementine. Ms. C will curl up in my lap when she feels up to the company. (Maybe I am dreaming about my future cat because Juvenile Court, otherwise a sanitized factory, smells distinctly of animal urine.) Ms. Clementine.

Sex was always the urge toward life after graduation, away from the same house we had always shared on the street of my childhood. Pimples and sweaty palms never got me hot enough to give up getting out of here and going Someplace to become a Somebody who could do Something.

Before my mom goes into the meeting, she sits next to me in the "privacy lounge." Her skin reflects a pallid glow sucked in from the overhead bank of lights. She talks to me, while I dumbly think: I am in juvenile court. Yes, we are here to undergo pre-trial talks with Weston's lawyer, which are supposed to be civil and fair. I am not on trial. I won't have to talk to Weston. I won't even see him. I'll stay right here on this vinyl seat and peruse *Good Housekeeping* for holiday baking ideas. I am tucked away in the bowels of the building; I am here with the criminals. Fear condenses in my armpits and I pull my jacket tight to ward off the damp chill.

My mom asks me again if I am okay. I say, Please go, and find out all that you can.

The shivers take over as she leaves me alone. I can endure this. This part is easy. I have Ms. Clementine to keep me company.

YOU SHOULD KNOW

The diner is empty tonight. I hear an old couple, loudly eating soft foods. Over there a spaghetti sauce encrusted toddler screams. The old couple lifts forkfuls of eggs in measured movements. The toddler's mom extends the juice cup.

Extract Bic, confront blank page, and write.

June 8th, 2002 is graduation day, which means I have 48 hours to write my salutatorian speech. Each time I sit down with Bic and paper, I get muddled up by the thought of standing there, my cap bobby-pinned to my hair at a precarious angle, while the crowd—teachers, students, parents, and hordes of visiting cousins who have been updated about *that* girl (me)—perch on the edges of their cold metallic chairs to hear me open my mouth to say, what? Thanks for the memories? The collected Grandma Smiths and assorted Aunt Sues will stare at me or whisper behind hands raised to cover their mouths. Fathers will shift and cross their arms over their broad chests.

What can I say to people who have decided I have nothing to say? Deep down I want them to see that I am good. I want them to understand that I was right to prosecute Weston.

Better to say the usual things and make it down the stairs without tripping on my heels. Better to be bland and tell them what they expect to hear.

I glance up and around the diner. And, click: I remember one rule about speaking is that you must consider the audience. The judgmental grandmas may be in the audience, but I don't want to say anything to them. Finally, I see my way into this speech. I will write my speech to Luke. He will be there. He will hear every word. At least he is supposed to be there.

The words start to flow. When I look up from my spiral notebook later, I see Ms. Turner, the counselor, and Ms. Walters, the English teacher, walking across the parking lot toward the diner. It's strange to see them outside of school. Their heads are bent close; they are not speaking in their teacher voices, which boom and direct and cajole when necessary. Ms. Turner holds the door for Ms. Walters and they step into my domain. I don't want them to catch me staring, so I pretend to read my notes as the host grabs menus and leads them to a table—my table.

"Okay," I say, "you can sit here." They ask about the coffee and dinner specials. I tell them the coffee is good and the pie is decent too. I can't give them advice about dinner, however. They decide to have breakfast-for-dinner: Denver omelets, whole-wheat toast (no butter), juice, and decaf coffee. When Ms. Walters asks about my notes, I tell her that I drafting my salutatory speech for graduation. She asks to see it and reads it, making messy notes in the margin.

I pour coffee into my mug, spilling a puddle into my

saucer, and try to act like this is normal. I am practically a high school graduate, and these women are not quite my teachers anymore. Except I don't know how to make small talk with teachers outside of the classroom. I tell Ms. Walters how much—Shakespeare, Whitman, Mother Jones—I learned in her class. She reassures me with a smile that she doesn't need me to say nice things about her class. She knows it is English and that not everyone thinks that English is as exciting as chemistry or ceramics or dragging Main Street or parties at the lake. (She didn't casually mention parties at the lake.) The air gets thin, and I think: intervention. They don't know what to order here, and yet they are at my table when they could have taken any number of open booths with views toward the road.

Ms. Turner eats her omelet with ketchup. They chat about school news, final essays to be graded, graduation, and summer vacations. Both plan to teach summer school. Between bites Ms. Turner tells me that the faculty board that determines the academic awards—including valedictorian and salutatorian—had a special meeting a few weeks ago. You know, she says, it is quite an honor to be awarded salutatorian. It was a very close race this year between you and Geoff Hickle in terms of grade-point average and overall academic achievement. The prize is first and foremost about grades, of course, and you were mere tenths of a point behind Geoff, she says. It turns out that five other students had tied with me for second place.

Why are they telling me this?

–We wanted you to win, Rebecca. You should know. You deserve to stand up and represent the best of your class.

There it is on the table.

I believe them without question or doubts. (I need to believe them.) I deserve the honor. Amazing. They cast their votes for me at the faculty meeting. Grace. Ms. Walters always pushed me in her class to do my "personal best." I knew she cared about my college essay and thought I had potential. I blew her off, mostly. And Ms. Turner was dating Ames (I thought), and here she is telling me that I did the right thing. They voted for me in the great faculty debate about the Class of 2002's best and brightest. I will stand up in front of my class not just because I worked my ass off and got the grades (at least up until this past semester) but also because I am the girl who did the brave thing, as far as these two women think. They came here to tell me.

–Wow, thanks.

They support me. They came here tonight to tell me. I feel a wave of gratitude wash over my sadness and dilute it. I needed this intervention. I don't understand how I deserve it or which Rebecca exactly they think I am. But it feels good to told that I am brave. I am brave, yes. That feels good to hear coming from a voice outside of my own head.

RAPE

The prosecutor, Mrs. Cruz, is fierce. Even though she was assigned to my case by default, she is committed to me.

She called to introduce herself and ask me questions, and she came to our house a few times. She always arrived on time and left on time. I found her terribly punctual and thought that this must be a good thing in a prosecutor, whose time is the taxpayer's dime (or so my mother informed me). She talked to my mom and dad while I hovered. I trusted her. It becomes easy to believe my story as I recount the details for her: He was popular and cute, he flirted with me, we both had a few drinks, and when I told him to stop, he wanted more and forced me. Against my will.

My mom respects her efficient manner, but trust might be a stretch. The minute the prosecutor steps out our front door and marches toward her no-nonsense sedan, Mom worries about the neighbors. She turns down reporters who call and leave messages asking her to please tell her daughter's side of the story. The newspapers don't use my name, but I almost wish they would print my name along with my picture. After all, I have done nothing wrong. I have nothing to hide.

The newspaper prints Weston's name, Weston Ames, in bold black font and uses his senior picture in color—the one with him smiling in a suit jacket and tie—every other day. His eyes are studious and serious, and a camera-perfect slow grin teases the corners of his mouth. A good sport. A kid. He looks like a parent's idea of the perfect prom date. *Home by curfew, sir.* My senior picture makes me look like a lawyer—good posture and intense eyes hard in my face with my hair pulled back in a low ponytail. I look like the kind of girl who would never cry wolf. I could give my permission for the paper to publish my picture, I'm told again and again. Yet it might look as if I want the attention. So I play the shrinking, faceless, voiceless victim.

The prosecutor stops by the Juvenile Court's privacy lounge on her way to the meeting with Ames, Weston, and the other lawyers. This afternoon her shoes are practical: soft leather Hush Puppies. She doesn't walk anywhere; rather, she seems to spread her wings and scamper along a lake surface to gain flight, her heavy hips ballast in the water and a powerful engine in flight. Heavy. Plodding. Like a goose. Yet ready to take flight. She means business. There is not a dust of powder of a hint of lipstick to smear her face. She wears her dark hair pulled too tightly into a bun. Her eyes bug from her forehead as she takes the waiting room in with a dismissive glance. She has been here before. She knows the stakes. She tells me straight what cards we've been dealt and how Weston's lawyer will try to get us to fold. Weston's lawyer will continue to plead not guilty.

No matter what, she says, remember that he is guilty and you are innocent.

What happens outside of the courtroom is irrelevant, she says.

She tells me to turn off any part of my brain that has been infected by rumor or fear or plain mean, ignorant gossip.

I turn off my brain. It's a matter of will. I blink my eyes, rub them like a child waking from a nap.

I open my eyes. My mom reappears from the bathroom, and we have a brief pow-wow of hushed voices right here in the lounge. When Mrs. Cruz says that the legal definition of what Weston did was *rape*, I know that she is absolutely correct. She tells us: It was not just a blowjob. It was forced penetration, which is rape. We will not settle for anything less, she tells us. My mom catches her breath and touches her hand to her mouth. She tells Mrs. Cruz that she had no idea the law backed up this kind of thing. (That is what she said, "this kind of thing.") She had thought Weston could only be punished for the physical assault and the threats. That may be the outcome, but we can still charge him with rape.

Mrs. Cruz asks if we are prepared to move forward with the rape charges. I nod and say, "Yes." (Yes. Finally, the law is getting it right. Weston is a rapist. Let's talk about that.) "Thank you, Mrs. Cruz."

My mom and Mrs. Cruz hug me and leave. I contemplate my arm hairs—so thick, so erratic—while I pretend to read dog-eared magazines with the recipes torn out.

While I turn page after page, I imagine the meeting:

Mom prickles along her spine when Weston and his dad enter the room with their lawyer. Mrs. Cruz matter-of-factly presents the charges, assault and rape.

Weston doesn't look at my mom when Cruz explicates the legal definition of *rape*.

His gaze is fixed to the tabletop between legal pads and errant pens and pencils, stealing glances at the clock above the door.

He knows that I know.

My only hope: he gets the stakes. If he denies my version of the attack, I will tell the press, the military recruiting officer, his dad, and the police that his real crime is something unspeakable—worse than just a blowjob after all.

He is perfectly screwed now.

His dad—freshly shaven and sharp in a button-down shirt and pinstriped tie—takes rapid-fire notes on a yellow legal pad. Ames will make a bulletproof plan to win. Hard work captures victory in every game—hardwood basketball court or courtroom. Homework counts. Honor is earned. Too bad he doesn't know the real pre-game statistics for his star athlete. Mrs. Cruz is a formidable coach in her own way, and she has the law on her side. Ames is outmatched.

I am sure.

GRADUATION DAY

I drive to Plains High School that morning for my passage out of childhood and into adulthood, supposedly. I avoid the rearview mirror.

Mom steam-ironed my gown and packed it in the backseat last night. Graduates are supposed to arrive early and get ready in the locker rooms. Mothers volunteered to be on hand to assist with bobby pins and torn pantyhose. I chose a simple black tunic dress to wear beneath the thin polyester graduation sheath. Later I will see that most of girls selected summer dresses in floral prints with embellishments of lace or complicated necklines. Tiffany's dress will be perfect: cream overlaid with a pale pink ruffle around the neck and hemline. She will look radiant. She will look like a girl going places.

When I tried on the black ensemble last night, my mother smiled and posed me in the kitchen. Despite the last few months, the official gown transformed me into a bona fide, high school graduate. I looked down the length of shimmering material with eyes that could cry at my own graduation, as if I were watching the event on an

274

after-school special or a big-screen Hollywood feature. If only I could be an observer of my own life, instead of an actor whose lines have not been memorized thoroughly.

My salutatorian's speech is typed in sizable font for easy reading and stowed in my purse. I practiced the speech on my mom while the gown fluttered about my knees and my cap balanced toward the back of my skull. She listened and clapped politely. I hope my audience will behave. Last night was awful as I imagined catcalls (or worse). What if everyone sits silent as stones when I finish? My mom will clap, I tell myself a thousand times. Moms will clap.

As I near the school I marvel at the blond brick walls, short and squat, appearing shorter and squatter than just yesterday. The parking lot is half-filled already, and a Sunday-dressed crowd has gathered near the driveway. With my eyes on their eager faces I nearly miss what drew them like hungry mosquitoes to the sidewalk. Black spray paint in free-spirited girlish curlicues spell out across the main drive:

We Love Weston! Class of '02 4-ever

4-ever. My skin ripples with gooseflesh, and then my stomach heaves with stomach acid mixed with Mom's cheesy scrambled eggs. The writing on the driveway. It has come to that. Of course. Years of decorating the star athletes' lockers for homecoming or hanging hand-painted signs on the gym walls to intimidate the rivals has instilled in our highly spirited gang of cheerleaders the art of public displays of affection, dedication, and whole-hearted team spirit.

Weston was allowed to earn his diploma in Juvenile Detention but was forbidden to attend graduation. Some students wrote letters of support to the school paper, which thankfully, I no longer had editorial power to accept or reject. He might not be here physically, yet each letter blackened on the pavement makes it clear that he is here in spirit. I might be here in body, but my classmates choose to exclude my spirit. I predicted averted eyes, efforts to avoid casual banter, no offers to adjust my tilted mortarboard. But this is worse than I expected. Just like that, I am erased from my own graduation day even as my flesh boils in the car.

So be it. I gather my purse and gown from the backseat. My black dress is dignified, understated, and appropriately funereal for this somber occasion.

POMP AND CIRCUMSTANCE

We stand two-by-two and wait for the marshal to cue our march. There is a collective silence. As the first half of the line snaked by us toward the entrance I see them: yellow high heels. Not only horrid fashion but nonregulation for graduation. The girls click hard against the linoleum as they pass me. They don't try to make eye contact with me to stick their point in my face. *Tie a yellow ribbon 'round an old oak tree* had become *wear hideous banana-yellow high heels*. Those girls, six of them, stand for Weston's return to his rightful place at our graduation. No one dares say this to my face. The girls' lips pull into tight, righteous lines as they file toward the doors.

I want to rip those hideous banana shoes off their feet and use them as weapons.

I fold and refold my speech into smaller half-sheets.

Luke files past me with a grin at odds with his glazed eyes and hands that fidget with his gown, his chin, and his collar in rhythmic obsession. He chucks me on the shoulder. He doesn't notice the girls in yellow shoes. He doesn't see much of anything these days. But he is here.

My audience of one. I've written the speech for him. I unfold the pages and smooth out the crease again. I refold it.

Our parents organized the final details of the graduation party for us. The invitations were mailed to relatives and a few teachers. Ms. Turner said to expect her. Ms. Walters will drop by with a card and a smile. She'll want to talk about my college plans and she'll tell me to let her know if I have any trouble writing on a collegiate level.

Yellow shoes. I didn't see that coming.

THE SPEECH

eye contact with Ms. Walters

Welcome, parents, family, and guests. In a few hours we, the class of 2002, will become citizens of the world.

deep breath

Thank you to our teachers. Although you gave us too much homework at times, Ms. Walters, and made us adhere to rules we didn't always agree with, Dean Hunter, without your tireless dedication and high standards of excellence, we would not be here before you today.

pause

I want to thank my mother, who loves me without question, and my father, whose support has been priceless.

longer pause

The class of 2002 sits here before you. We look more grown up than we did when we first entered this building four years ago. I have known most of my fellow classmates since seventh grade. Together we forged our own path toward this graduation day.

Some of us are star athletes, some are genius scholars,

some excelled in theater, and some excelled in extracurricular activities. We each have our talents and strengths.

The events of this year, the terrible fall of the twin towers far away in New York City together with the lessons we have learned here in the hallways of PHS, have taught us the difference between right and wrong. As President Bush says, "There can be no neutrality between justice and cruelty, between the innocent and the guilty. We are in a conflict between good and evil, and America will call evil by its name." This is a powerful idea. There is no neutrality between the innocent and the guilty. This means that we must choose a side, we must choose between good and evil and dare to speak. We must call evil by its name.

pause

We take our personal talents with us to face the future and do battle with evil. As we go forward, we keep in mind that strength leads to success and along with it a great responsibility to make the world better, to protect those we love, to defend our freedom.

pause *eye contact* *pause*

I want to make the world a better place. I want the world to be safe, to be filled with kindness, and defined by truth. In the end success is measured by how we have cared for one another.

When I was a sophomore, I discovered the poems of Emily Dickinson. I used to carry around one of her poems in my pocket. I want to share it with you today because her words about friendship are true. As Emily Dickinson says,

I'm Nobody! Who are you?

Are you – Nobody – Too?

Then there's a pair of us!

Don't tell! they'd advertise – you know!

In these lines she says it's okay to let others think you are a Nobody—as long as you have a friend to share your good and bad times with. Her poem goes on to say,

How dreary – to be – Somebody!

How public – like a Frog –

To tell one's name – the livelong June –

To an admiring Bog!

In these lines she tells us that being a "Somebody" in this world can be dreary and tiresome if you have to constantly be on public display.

pause

This poem tells me that it is better to keep our friends safe, even as we add new ones, and to use our strengths and talents for our friends instead of striving for wealth or popularity. In this way we can be our own star. In this way we shine with the light of truth. In this way we are free.

pause

And so this the last homework assignment: We are sent forth to do our best to make this beautiful and terrifying world better than it is now. And in doing we should keep our friends close to our hearts, even if the world may see you as less than a Somebody with a capital S.

pause

Soon the class of 2002 will be no more; we will be "alumni." We will hang up our letter jackets. We will move on to so-called real life. We should be a light for the world—to illuminate the dark times. May we always welcome true friends home with open arms.

pause

Thank you.

I didn't stumble or drop my speech. My hands did shake. I kept them pressed flat to the podium, nailing my pages in place. I had to bend my knees to regain my sense of balance, twice. I must believe that Luke will hear what I said beneath the platitudes. *May we always welcome true friends home with open arms.* I have to believe he'll hold my words in his heart.

I made my case. I stood my ground at the speaker's podium, the witness stand. I kept my chin up. I talked the talk. Now I will walk the walk. I have no choice but to move on. Move away. Go to college. Become Somebody. Else. But no matter who that girl will be, Luke, please know: My arms will always be wide open. *Then there's a pair of us!*

DIPLOMA

Three steps up. The metal stairs sway beneath me. Five steps. Reach with the left. Shake with right. Pause for the camera. Smile. Five steps. Three steps down. A small red leather book in my hands, inside is the diploma.

The replacement for Principal Ames shakes my hand and offers me the diploma. In the burst of the camera's flash, I understand that no one can ever take it away from me. It is so much more than a piece of paper. It is my ticket. Nonreturnable. No exchanges.

I wonder if Luke's red leather case is empty. He smiles for the photographer all the same.

GREEN JEEP WOMAN

Mom insists we meet at the house after graduation so
we can drive to Luke's house together for the party. The
thought of being her ride home makes me less than
happy—no escape route in case I need to bail out from my
own party. I coast into the driveway, gather my bags and
assorted graduation flotsam, and plod toward the front
door. I am relieved to have the ceremony done. Now there
is the party.

I fumble through the unlocked front door and shout
that I'm home. My mom says, Hello, Rebecca from the
living room couch. I jump out of my skin. She never sits
there unless she is zoned out by the television, which is
dead stone silent now. She has that goofy I've-got-a-
surprise-for-you grin. That sweet smile triggers chemicals
that burst through my cell walls and cancel my drudgery.
My head detaches from my body. Her glowy face daubed
with pale pink blusher together with her excited straight
spine radiate good news; nevertheless, I fear what will
come out her mouth. I don't trust her body language. She
must know. Luke told. Weston told. I am found out. The

whole twisted game is up and my carefully cultivated suffering is a wasted effort.

I want to drop my armload of stuff and run. Instead I raise an eyebrow and find an available finger to scratch at my nose.

–Rebecca, honey, hello? Did you happen to notice anything on your way into the house?

My crinkled graduation gown spills to the floor with my bag as I tell her that I guess I was too busy trying to carry my stuff in to the house. She tells me to take a look. I walk out the front door and there she is: My Jeep. My mom comes up behind me and squeezes my shoulders, pressing the car keys into my hand.

–It's all yours.

I turn to her and let her arms hold me close.

–You deserve it, honey.

HUG

My mom wants Luke and me to pose with the cake. We move behind the table and he pulls me next to him. We turn toward the room filled with cameras and open our eyes wide toward the flash of lights and shouts for our attention.

Luke stands next to me as I begin to slice into the cake. Before long Luke's mom takes over my clumsy attempts to transfer slices onto floppy paper plates. Luke takes my hand, and I follow him through the crowd. Our hands fit together, his fingers gently tugging me along with him down the hall and through the front door. Outside it is quiet. The crowd a world away inside the house. We stand in the corner of the yard, under the apple tree that no longer flowers in the spring.

I don't wait for him to say a word. What can he say? What can I say? I put my arms around him and press my face into his chest. He hugs me, his hands smooth down my hair and press into my shoulders. We breathe. I smell the sugar from the frosting. I rest in his arms. I don't think. I am happy for just this moment. And then I pull away.

–Thanks for the party.

–You're welcome.

It is our last embrace. We both know it.

EPILOGUE

COFFEE. PLAIN.

I hung up the phone. Immediately I type a regretful letter to decline the internship "due to family health issues." I send a copy to my professor as well, knowing full well that I am a coward not to pick up the phone and tell him. I don't know how to explain my sudden allegiance to a mother he has never heard me mention. My personal life is not a topic discussed in seminar, and it embarrasses me to imagine how I would phrase my mother's continued grief at the loss of her mother. My grandmother.

My mom's shattered bravery was in her voice. I heard her sadness despite her valiant attempt to protect my best interests. Kansas City and the internship with the law firm will have to wait. My mom needs me to say nothing, to hold her hand. She needs me to sleep until noon and work a part time job at the mall. She needs me to eat dinner with her. To sit across the table while she talks about her day. This I can do. This one thing I learned from the disaster of my high school days. When someone who loves you calls, you show up.

Better yet, you only show up. Say nothing, do nothing.

Just show up.

It's not easy to spend the entire summer in my hometown.

Here I am, back at the diner, the restaurant of my high school angst. It is the same four walls, the same revolving pie case, and the same vacuum cleaner. I don't recognize the manager, but people move on. No one recognizes me. I am not even *that* girl anymore, perhaps, nearly three years later.

Despite the hum of fluorescent lights and the noise of diners deep into mountains of eggs and bacon, my life in college is more real to me than this place. I am in a movie here. This diner feels like a stage set. I go through the scene, following my stage directions. Except there are no cameras here. The audience is not watching me. I am not the center of the show.

The ordeal, as I call it, the carnage and yellow high heels of my senior year, demanded its price as the days turned to months and then three Christmas trips to Florida. I am junior now at KU. Truth: It got easier to live without Luke, it became possible to live with myself. I survive. I go through the motions. I bide my time. I don't write my personal-goal lists. I do. I do what I am told. Study, study, study. I am polite. Cold. Grown up.

College life—new people, new places, new spiral notebooks with crisp blue lines to fill with careful lecture notes during Art History and Chemistry and Sociology— has given me a way forward. A way to endure. My grownup life is life without my best friend. I accept who I have become: a person whose capacity for pure, unfiltered romantic love is used up and shut down by my own volition. My fault. Who I am, the sum of my actions.

Tiffany and I travel in different circles at KU. She remains a good friend to me. But we are not close anymore. We meet for coffee sometimes. Freshman year I took a single dorm room. She was placed in a triple suite and within weeks she was part of a triplet—Tiffy, Shan, Jen. They are joined at the hip. They were meant for each other. She never fails to hug me when we pass in the halls. I am happy for her. She is a free spirit.

Grandma is gone. Grandma lived alone, happily, in her condo, as long as I knew her. I long for her simple dinners, her quiet days, her contained life bordered by the ocean. But our winter trips to Florida are over now.

At college I manage to be Rebecca New, Rebecca White, a blank sheet. In Florida, however, for a few weeks each year, I always gave into the lure of the brine in the air and sand in my hair. In Florida I succumbed to the memories, knowing that when Christmas break ended I would return to classes and do what I was told. In Florida I took long walks alone and talked to Luke. I would tell him I hadn't betrayed him. I accepted his tearful gratitude. I held his hand. I let him kiss me on the forehead as the sun set in glorious orange and pink bursts. We sat together in the sand and counted the hard, white pebbles. The sand shifted through our palms in endless streams. In my imagination, I let myself be with Luke. Being with him in my daydreams in Florida taught me tenderness toward him, even a tenderness with myself. I learned to live with the truth. It cannot be undone. At the end of break, it was always back to the books. Study the law. Smile at appropriate times. Stay awake.

Since high school, the trips to Florida recalled my childhood self—a girl going places, a girl who believed in, well, believing. As we neared the coast each winter, the sense of what was real slipped away from me. Possibilities teemed on the horizon. But I am no longer the same girl who believed in the Atlantic Ocean as if it were my primal home. When I learned in seventh grade that the Kansas plains used to be an ocean floor, I created my myth as a child born to the Kansas plains yet tied to the ancient ocean that had once filled the heartland. I was born of Kansas and her fragrant harvests, and Kansas was born of the oceans. When my feet pressed into the sand suffused with ocean life, I saw myself as an ancient as-yet-unworshipped goddess whose tread would someday be the ground for a new geography. The coast would give way to the plains, given enough time and the inexplicable works of the wind and tides. I felt privy to this wisdom and touched by the grandeur of my insight. That Rebecca was definitely Rebecca Before.

There will be no more trips to Florida—at least, not to stay with Grandma.

Mom plans to rent Grandma's condo. She wants to sell our house. Mom needs me to pack up everything and get it ready for showings. She'll rent an apartment near her office until she retires. It's too soon, she says, to retire. She can't bear the thought of sitting idle with no income, at least not yet.

My brain shut down when I saw the boxes and the massive weight of delicate porcelain figurines waiting for me to wrap them in newspaper and bury them deep in boxes marked *fragile*. I needed calories to move just one of them. My jeep hit the road and moved in a straight line toward the diner. My hands directed the wheel, made crucial left and right turns. My feet worked the pedals. My brain pretended to operate in the forgiving realm of the subconscious. I found myself at the diner by accident (on purpose). The booth sagged to meet me.

Grandma died four months ago. She had a massive stroke in her sleep. The doctors told mom that she passed peacefully without pain or suffering or fear. She must have performed her nightly ritual with serene indifference to the imminent betrayal of her own brain. She washed her face with a damp, soapy cloth, applied creams and powders. She pulled her thin Florida nightgown over her head and settled it against her breasts and thighs. She read a chapter of her current mystery novel (I hope it was the last chapter) and turned out the bedside lamp with never a thought to the dignity of her deathbed drama. She went gently into the night.

Or did she? Was she anxious or crabby or overwhelmed by a black fear unnamed hovering on the edge of her evening? Did death tug at her brocaded bed cover with teasing fingers? I think of her more than I would have been able to predict. I see her taking a warm casserole from the oven with two big pristine oven mitts. She doesn't hurry or comment on the aroma. I see her driving us through the warm Florida air pushing the gas pedal to the speed limit to beat the setting sun. I put her arms around me in a firm hug—an embrace that communicates deeper than sentiment and stronger than words. She is with me in the diner now. She would order the chef salad, dressing on the side. I order the same thing.

Rummaging through my bag, I extract my Bic and a legal pad. My hands work to arrange a fresh page and move my pen in sharp circles on a napkin to draw forth the ink. I am home again in the diner. I came home, and the town remains tidy-lawned and languid. The wide roads and minivans throb with veiled domestic drama right before my eyes.

My head might just explode with the fourth dimension as time folds and unfolds inside the grease-stained atmosphere of this run-down restaurant.

Mom asked me to buy packing peanuts and industrial-strength garbage bags. I want to go by the school and see Ms. Walters, my high school English teacher. I need to mail some checks to pay my rent and utilities. I want to go to the post office and apply for a passport.

I drink my coffee plain, and alone.

At school I check in at the Main Office. Ms. Walters is not there, but she left me a manila envelope. I restrain a nostalgic urge to roam the halls, breathe in the scent of linoleum wax. I head back to my car with the package clutched in my hand, eager to open it.

I shake the contents onto the passenger seat. There are two letters, one addressed to me in my own handwriting. The other is addressed to me in Luke's handwriting. This was Ms. Walters' assignment, but the letters are early. Her note explains that she sent them now because she's taking a leave of absence to care for her daughter. She hasn't opened the letters and has no idea why Luke addressed his letter to me, but she trusts that Luke must have intended for me to read it. Perhaps I should read it and then deliver it to Luke, she suggests.

I can't open the letters in the sunstroke heat of my jeep. It is neither the place nor the time. I watch the freshman tennis team leave the front door and head toward the courts for summer practice. Their shoes gleam new and white in the afternoon sun. I prepare for what the letters might contain. I remember the hard slanting cursive of Luke's handwriting. It slays me to think of him writing to himself after it had happened and before the party at Weston's house that Spring Break.

I don't open the letters, not yet. Instead I help my mother sort and pack the rest of the afternoon and into the evening. At ten o'clock we call it quits and I take the excuse for a long shower. When I emerge dripping and calmed by the hot water, my mom has already gone to bed. I hit the road with the letters. I drive past Luke's old house where his parents still manage the chaos of who knows how many kids. The lights are on, and I consider stopping by, but how can you say hello after all these years? Small talk is impossible.

I pull into an empty parking lot in a deserted park and cut the engine. I open my letter first. I remember writing for the entire hour and then trashing my draft and writing the final letter just before the bell rang. The one-page handwritten letter is 100-percent bland: I dreamed of a not-too-distant college graduation, with a "great" boyfriend. I hoped to have a "great" major like journalism or history or biology. I hoped that my dad is "great" and that my mom has retired to Florida after winning the lottery. *Great.* You would think that four years of English would have given me a more descriptive way to dream my future life. I managed to say nothing, even though I remember such determination when I scrawled my letter to my imaginary future self. I even made sure to pass Luke an envelope and stamp during passing period, I remember. He grabbed it from me and stuffed into his backpack.

I slit the envelope for Luke's letter with a fingernail. As

I remove the letter, I admit that I have no intention of showing him the letter while hoping that it will give me a valid reason to track him down and deliver it, face to face. I have never dared to find him even though I know I could. It is far too easy to do damage in the name of love. I am not sure what I want to do after college, how I will earn my living, spend my life. But there are a few things I am sure that I do not want: I do not want to inflict more damage on Luke or scare him away forever. The timing has to be precisely cosmic for our reunion. I am sure it will happen one day when it is supposed to happen. And not before.

There is a single sheet of notebook paper inside the envelope. I hold my breath and unfold it. It is perfectly blank. Not a Dear Luke, or even a Dear Rebecca. No erasure marks. Not one single word. I am tricked up, I think, our high school lingo. I trace the empty lines. Tricked up. I turn the page over and back again. Blank. Truth: He left it blank, and addressed it to me. How eloquent. He is a true poet.

Later that summer, I bump into some kids from school. Their smiles are wide. They seem warm and forgiving. It must be that merciful forgetfulness that blossoms after enough time has passed. It causes them forget who they used to be, the kind of person who scorned me even as they hated their own seething self-doubt and boiling false bravado.

I meet their eyes and discover I can ask,

–Whatever happened to Luke Warren?

Truth: Luke got married to Jenni from KanMart. It wasn't too long after graduation, in fact. Last anyone heard, he is still the manager at a new diner in the next town over. Been at least two years now since they moved there. He has two kids, two girls.

(I don't ask about Weston. No one mentions his name to me. Principal Ames stepped down the following year. They moved out of state.)

One Wednesday night at supper, over chicken with rice, mom mentions that she ran into Luke last August at the grocery store. He asked how I was doing and told her to tell me hi. Just that, hi, she says. It had slipped her mind, she says. But Luke seemed real happy. Real happy, she says.

I say, Okay.

I can't say, That is real good.

I say nothing. I keep my promise. I watch. I study. I breathe. I wait. Truth, Dare, Promise. No Repeats.

I say, "Mom, I love you."

She smiles, a brave smile, and we hold hands across the table for a moment. She pulls her hand away to pick up her napkin and wipe crumbs into her hand.

ACKNOWLEDGEMENTS

This book is a product of my belief in justice which was instilled by my parents. For this I am grateful to Ronald and Lovella Kelley.

My commitment to women's rights and my activism to create a violence-free world were inspired by my Catholic education and my formation as a thinker at a women's college, Saint Mary's College. V's *The Vagina Monologues* gave me the chance to connect with a wonderful group of peers who continue to inspire me to listen to those who have been silenced. This book is a tribute to those teachers, authors, and activists who shaped my vision.

This text has evolved thanks to many readers, including Deborah Justice and Gail Mandell who were among the first and the most thoughtful to respond.

I am grateful to my circle of friends and to my book clubs. Without the insight and inspiration of the following women, this book would have stayed in a drawer: Elly Wynia, Akesha Baron, Modla Zsuzsanna, Lou Irwin, Mary Nicolini, Mary Malloy, Lisa Nóvé, Palya Bea, Colleen Erickson, Teagan Knecht Pandy, Székely Orsolya, Allison Hastings, Tina Thompson, Ashley Ratcliffe Beumer, Joanne Lowery, Julia Kerner, and Julia Africa.

Jason Dinges, a true friend, cheers me on from heaven. This is not his story.

Thank you to Nick Courtright, Alexis Kale, and the team at Atmosphere Press for their patience and attention to detail that made this story into a book on the shelf for readers.

And finally I am grateful for my husband, Barabási Albert-László, who inspired me to become an artist on my own terms. To my three children, Daniel, Iza and Leo, my best creations, may you be hungry to make art in a world changed forever by the Covid-19 pandemic. Sheltering with you has softened my edges. And to Miss Mary, our rescue dog who rescued us, you are a terrible dog but a perfect addition to our family.

ABOUT ATMOSPHERE PRESS

Atmosphere Press is an independent, full-service publisher for excellent books in all genres and for all audiences. Learn more about what we do at atmospherepress.com.

We encourage you to check out some of Atmosphere's latest releases, which are available at Amazon.com and via order from your local bookstore:

The Embers of Tradition, a novel by Chukwudum Okeke

Saints and Martyrs: A Novel, by Aaron Roe

When I Am Ashes, a novel by Amber Rose

Melancholy Vision: A Revolution Series Novel, by L.C. Hamilton

The Recoleta Stories, by Bryon Esmond Butler

Voodoo Hideaway, a novel by Vance Cariaga

Hart Street and Main, a novel by Tabitha Sprunger

The Weed Lady, a novel by Shea R. Embry

A Book of Life, a novel by David Ellis

It Was Called a Home, a novel by Brian Nisun

Grace, a novel by Nancy Allen

Shifted, a novel by KristaLyn A. Vetovich

Because the Sky is a Thousand Soft Hurts, stories by Elizabeth Kirschner

ABOUT THE AUTHOR

Janet Kelley is a teacher, reader, writer, and feminist. A native of Hutchinson, Kansas, she studied Humanistic Studies and Religious Studies at Saint Mary's College, Notre Dame, Indiana. She studied Historical Theology at the University of Notre Dame. She earned her teaching credentials from Indiana University at South Bend. Ms. Kelley currently lives in Boston and Budapest.

Ms. Kelley believes that books are the cornerstone of freedom and justice. Her work to support survivors of sexual assault was inspired by the writer V and *The Vagina Monologues*. A portion of the proceeds from the sale of this novel will be donated to The Trevor Project. Please consider a donation to The Trevor Project to support their crisis intervention and suicide prevention services for LGBTQ youth.

You can connect with Janet on Twitter at @hutchkelley5.